A LUCKY ESCAPE

"Hey, Callie," Carole said, "I didn't know you were coming on the trail ride with us."

"Neither did I," Callie replied grimly, willing herself not to look back. "It was sort of a last-minute change of plans."

She didn't explain further. She couldn't bring herself to get into the whole story just then.

"Well, we're glad you could come along," Stevie said carefully. "Um, but do you think that George wanted to—"

"I'm sick of George Wheeler!" Callie snapped before her friend could finish her sentence. "If I had to spend a whole trail ride with him, I'd probably puke."

She realized that her friends might think she was acting like a jerk, but she didn't care. They weren't the ones who had to deal with George every time they turned around. They weren't the ones who spent every day kicking themselves for ever letting him into their lives. They couldn't possibly understand what that was like. So they could simply think whatever they wanted to think. Callie was just glad she'd escaped this time.

**Don't miss any of the excitement
at PINE HOLLOW,
where friends come first:**

And coming in April 2001:

PINE HOLLOW®

TRACK RECORD

BY BONNIE BRYANT

BANTAM BOOKS
NEW YORK • TORONTO • LONDON • SYDNEY • AUCKLAND

Special thanks to Laura Roper and Sir "B" Farms

RL 5.0, AGES 012 AND UP

TRACK RECORD
A Bantam Book/February 2001

ISBN: 0-553-49360-4

Visit us on the Web! www.randomhouse.com
Educators and librarians, for a variety of teaching tools, visit us at
www.randomhouse.com/teachers

Published simultaneously in the United States and Canada

Bantam Books is an imprint of Random House Children's Books. BANTAM
BOOKS and the rooster colophon are registered trademarks of Random
House, Inc. Bantam Books, 1540 Broadway, New York, New York 10036.

PRINTED IN THE UNITED STATES OF AMERICA

OPM   10 9 8 7 6 5 4 3 2 1

My special thanks to Catherine Hapka
for her help
in the writing of this book.

ONE

Callie Forester sat on the sofa, clutching the armrest so hard that her fingers were numb. It felt like forever since her older brother had rushed out of the room into the dark January night, though in reality it had only been a minute or two. What was taking Scott so long? What had he found out there? Was *he* in danger? Should she call the police, go outside herself, *do* something, anything?

Chill, Callie told herself sternly, taking a few deep breaths. *You recognized that face at the window just now. You know who it was, and there's no way Scott's in any danger from him.*

Somehow, the thought wasn't particularly comforting. Why hadn't she told her brother the truth? Chewing on her lower lip and tugging on the end of her straight blond hair, Callie stood up and sidled toward the window. The moon was hidden behind a thick layer of clouds, and the front yard was dark, full of deep shadows and uncertain shapes.

Callie jumped as the front door swung open and Scott hurried in, his face red from the winter cold. "Nobody out there," he reported breathlessly, slapping his arms across his chest to warm himself. "Whoever you saw must've taken off when he heard me coming."

Callie was strangely relieved. She was already wishing she had just kept her mouth shut in the first place. If she hadn't been so startled by the sight of that face, she could have dealt with it on her own instead of dragging her brother into it. "Oh well," she said, doing her best to keep her voice normal. "It was probably just some neighborhood kid playing a prank, like you said."

"I'm not so sure about that," Scott said slowly, glancing at the darkness beyond the picture window. "I found a footprint right outside the window there. It was kind of hard to see in the dark, but it was definitely too big to belong to a kid. It looks like we're dealing with a full-grown Peeping Tom."

"Oh." Callie wanted to argue with him, to insist that it had all been nothing. A little kid playing some silly spy game. A particularly bold deer or stray dog. A figment of her imagination.

And maybe that last one is the truth, she told herself. *Maybe I'm so jumpy about all this that now I'm imagining things.*

It wasn't the first time that possibility had crossed

her mind. In the past weeks she had often wondered if she might not be losing it, seeing things that weren't there and assuming things that just couldn't be.

But she couldn't quite dismiss the image burned into her brain—the sight of an all-too-familiar face, pale and round and apple-cheeked, pressing against the glass, its watery gray eyes fixed on her.

George Wheeler's face. It had definitely been George out there. Or was she so certain? Had everything that had happened lately made her so jumpy that she couldn't even trust her own senses anymore? After all, George had made her feel a little off balance from the beginning. Even months ago, when she'd thought his crush on her was harmless and sweet, she'd never been sure how to respond to him. He was so different from most guys—helpless and gentle and almost painfully sensitive. Or at least that was what she'd thought until recently.

"I sort of think we should call someone," Scott said. "Maybe the police? Or we could try to reach Mom and Dad at the country club." He seemed uncertain, which wasn't a familiar state with him. Callie sometimes thought that Scott had been born knowing exactly what to say and do in every possible situation. She assumed he'd inherited that particular talent from their father, a congressman and a natural-born politician. Seeing Scott flounder made Callie feel even worse about the whole situation and guilty that she'd let things with George progress this far.

"Don't be silly," she insisted quickly. "I'm not even sure I saw anything. It could've been a reflection from headlights on the road or something."

"But the footprint—" Scott began, glancing anxiously toward the window.

"That footprint could be days old," Callie interrupted. "It's probably yours." She forced a laugh. "Let's not get too hysterical here, okay?"

Scott shook his head, still looking worried. "I don't know, Callie," he said slowly. "It could be nothing. But Dad's made some real enemies because of his work on that congressional welfare committee this fall. I still think we should—"

"There's no need to get Dad involved in this," Callie broke in sharply.

"Get me involved in what?"

Callie gulped. She had been so busy trying to convince Scott to let the whole incident drop that she hadn't heard the front door open. She glanced into the hall and saw her parents unwrapping their winter scarves and coats and shaking off the cold.

Callie's mother pulled off her hat and ran one slender hand over her smooth blond hair. Stepping forward into the living room, she glanced around, a look of dismay on her fine-boned face. "Oh my!"

she said. "What's going on? This place looks like a disaster!"

Callie winced, suddenly remembering the mess she'd made. She had fixed herself a snack just before the peeping incident and ended up dropping it when she'd seen the face pressed to the window. Now she realized that strawberry yogurt was seeping into the Oriental rug in front of the sofa and grapes were rolling around on the hardwood floor.

"Callie saw someone," Scott said before she could open her mouth. "Like a Peeping Tom or something. There's a footprint outside the window."

Congressman Forester looked concerned. "Callie, is this true?"

"Well . . ." Callie hesitated, but she knew better than to lie to her father. "Um, sort of. I mean, I thought I saw someone—er, something—at the window. But I'm not sure it was really a Peeping Tom," she added hastily. "I didn't get a good look."

"Oh dear," Mrs. Forester said, glancing at her husband. "Do you suppose we should call someone?"

"I don't know." Congressman Forester took a step toward the window, peering out into the darkness. "Maybe I should go out and take a look around."

Callie bit her lip, wishing again that none of this was happening. The last thing she wanted was to let her parents make a big deal out of this stupid incident. All that would do would be to make it more difficult than ever to put it all behind her.

"Scott already looked and there's no one there," she said, feeling rather desperate. "Really, I'm not even sure I saw anyone. It was just out of the corner of my eye. There's no reason to get all worked up about this."

To her surprise, her father nodded. "All right," he said. "I suppose we can just turn on the alarm and keep a close eye on things for a few days."

Callie let out the breath she was holding. "Good," she said. Turning away to hide the relief on her face, she added, "Don't worry, I'll clean up the mess."

"Don't bother with that." Mrs. Forester was already bending to gather up the stray grapes. "I'll take care of it. Whatever happened, you must have had quite a scare, and it's late. Why don't you head up to bed?"

"Okay." Callie didn't have to be told twice. "Thanks, Mom. See you in the morning."

She headed for the stairs before her family could ask any more questions. Moments later she was collapsing onto her bed, wondering how she'd ever gotten mixed up with George Wheeler in the first place.

But she already knew the answer to that. It was all

her fault. Everything had happened because she had let it happen. She had allowed him to think they were friends—even to hope they could be something more—merely because she had assumed he was nothing more than a clueless dork. Her first mistake had been agreeing to go out with him once. After that one date she had made her second big mistake. Even though she'd known by then that there was no way she would ever be romantically interested in him, she hadn't just come right out and said so. Why not? She still wasn't sure.

I guess I'm not the only one who's ever assumed things about George because of the way he looks, she reminded herself, thinking about people at Pine Hollow, the stable where they both rode. George was way too pudgy and unkempt-looking to inspire much awe in his competition even in the relatively casual eventing world. In fact, most people who saw him on the ground never imagined that he could be any kind of athlete. But Callie had seen him ride often enough to know that in his case, appearances were deceiving. He was one of the best young riders at Pine Hollow. Callie had never seen him compete, but she knew from hearing her friends talk that George was a talented eventer, competing and winning at training level.

None of that made her feel much better about her own situation, though. If only she hadn't misjudged

George, the way so many of his fellow event-ers must have done over the years, maybe she wouldn't be in this mess. But she was in it now, and moving forward would be a lot more productive than looking back and wishing she could change what had already happened. She had learned that in her own competitive career in endurance riding.

Now all she had to do was figure out how to move on.

"Justine!" Carole Hanson exclaimed cheerfully. "Hey there! How's it going?"

"Fine." Justine Harrington shot Carole a slightly suspicious look, then scurried off in the direction of the tack room.

Carole grinned. She had spent much more time yelling at the stubborn seventh-grade riding student about accepting the horse she was assigned and not running in the stable than showering her with happy greetings. It was no wonder the younger girl had just looked at her as if she were crazy. But Car-ole couldn't help herself. Even though she'd been riding a few times a week recently, it was a whole different feeling to be returning to work after almost two months off. It was like coming home. Even the most obnoxious intermediate riders felt like long-lost family.

Hesitating in the center of the stable's roomy entryway, Carole glanced in one direction and then the other, pulling indecisively on her thick black braid. She knew she should head down the hall to the office, but she couldn't resist turning the other way and walking down the wide stable aisle. Before she got down to work, there were a few friends she wanted to see.

It was early, and most of the horses were still munching on their morning meal. As she rounded the corner, Carole saw a large roan head peering at her from behind the metal mesh of the top half of the nearest stall door. "Hey there, Checkers," she said, poking her fingers through to stroke the sturdy school horse on his mottled nose.

Carole moved on, pausing just long enough to pat a boarder's Tennessee walking horse before stopping in front of another stall. A compact leopard Appaloosa gelding blinked at her and then came forward to greet her.

"Hi, Scooby," Carole said as the horse blew gently on her fingers with his wide nostrils. She gave him a few pats and scratches, watching him carefully to figure out which were his favorite areas. Scooby was Callie Forester's horse, and he was new to Pine Hollow—in fact, he'd moved in only two weeks earlier. Callie had been a junior endurance champion on the West Coast and had planned to continue the sport after her family had moved to Virginia the previous summer. Unfortunately, a serious car accident had put those plans on hold for a while. Callie had spent most of the past six months in physical therapy, regaining her balance and her confidence. But now that Callie was better, Carole knew, she had to be eager to get back into the swing of things. She had made a good start by buying Scooby. Carole didn't know as much about endurance riding as she did about some other riding sports, but she knew enough to realize that Scooby had the appropriate conformation and temperament for the task.

As Carole was leaning on the stall door, studying Scooby's nicely sloping shoulders, Maureen Chance came barreling around the corner, pushing a wheelbarrow full of grain buckets. She stopped short and grinned when she spotted Carole. "Hey, Hanson," she said. "If this is how hard you always work, I don't know if I should say welcome back or not."

Carole returned Maureen's grin. "You're starting to sound just like Max," she teased in return.

Maureen rolled her gold-flecked brown eyes toward the ceiling. "Say it ain't so. I hope I'm never that old."

Carole blinked, wondering if Maureen realized that her comment came across as obnoxious rather than funny. The twenty-five-year-old stable hand had started working at Pine Hollow just a couple of weeks earlier, and Carole still wasn't sure what to think of her. There was a certain quality in the way she carried herself, a kind of hardness that made Carole a little nervous sometimes. But at the moment, even Maureen's sarcastic sense of humor couldn't dampen her own good mood. "Anyway, you're right," Carole said. "I'd better get cracking. I just need to check on Starlight first."

As Maureen continued on her way, Carole hurried down the aisle to a stall near the middle. The tall bay gelding inside came forward at her step and greeted her with a nicker.

"Hey, boy," Carole murmured. Tears sprang to her eyes. As much as she had missed everything about spending time at Pine Hollow, she didn't realize until that moment just how hard it had been to be separated from her horse, only seeing him for a limited number of hours per week and being forced to leave him almost exclusively to the care of other people for the first time since she'd owned him. She quickly unlatched the stall door and slid inside, wrapping her arms around Starlight's neck.

She was a little surprised to find herself getting so choked up as the gelding nosed at her hair, blowing warm breath on her neck under her braid. True, she had missed her horse a lot. True, she was really glad to be back, finished with being grounded and all the

11

rest of it. Still, she suspected that her sudden rush of emotions might also have something to do with something else, something that had happened two nights earlier on New Year's Eve.

She pushed that idea out of her mind as quickly as it had come. She didn't want to think about Cam Nelson right then. Stroking Starlight's face, she took a few deep breaths and did her best to get her emotions under control.

Carole jumped when she heard someone clear his throat in the aisle outside. Spinning around, she saw Ben Marlow watching her.

"Oh!" Carole blushed immediately, though she wasn't sure why. It wasn't as though she needed to be embarrassed that Ben had caught her hugging and patting her horse. Ben would be the last person in the world to criticize or make fun of something like that—most people who met Ben soon realized that he seemed to like horses better than people. That quality was one of the first things Carole had appreciated about him when he'd started working at Pine Hollow a couple of years earlier. It was sometime after that that she'd begun noticing that Ben had other attributes, as well. Like broad shoulders and deep, somber brown eyes—eyes that were gazing at her steadily at that very moment.

"Um, h-hi," Carole stammered, not knowing what else to say. Unbidden, a rush of memories

12

from New Year's Eve flooded her mind. A lot of them were awful, painful memories having to do with Cam, the guy who'd pursued her and then dumped her. But a few featured Ben, who had been there afterward.

"Welcome back." Ben was staring over her shoulder at Starlight. He cleared his throat. "Um, Starlight will be glad to have you around full-time again."

Carole smiled tentatively. Ben usually didn't have much to say, and she was a little surprised that he was actually standing there making small talk. Of course, she'd been more than a little surprised on New Year's Eve, too, when he'd asked her to dance. Was he turning over a new leaf? Or was this just a fluke—like the time a couple of months earlier when he'd kissed her and then pretended it never happened?

"I'm glad to be back," she said lightly, though her cheeks were still burning.

"Well." Ben paused. Keeping his gaze fixed on Starlight, who was nuzzling Carole's shoulder, he said, "Uh, so Starlight looks good. Um . . ."

Carole could tell he was casting around for something else to say. She wanted to help him, but her mind was suddenly a total blank. What did people say to each other, anyway? She couldn't imagine.

"Carole!" Max Regnery exclaimed heartily, appearing from around the corner of the aisle. "Welcome back!"

Carole turned to watch as the stable owner hurried toward them, a broad smile lighting his blue eyes and weather-beaten face. Max had inherited Pine Hollow from his late father, who had taken it over from his father before him. Max ran the stable with strict discipline, a sense of humor, and a deep and genuine love of horses and riders alike. The place was in his blood, and Carole couldn't imagine him doing anything else. His older daughter, five-year-old Maxine, had clearly inherited the family love of horses, and Carole could already picture the little girl taking the reins someday and carrying on the Pine Hollow tradition for another generation.

"Thanks!" Carole smiled at Max, doing her best to ignore the fact that Ben was slinking away down the aisle. Was he relieved that Max had interrupted? Or disappointed? She tried not to wonder. "It's great to be here," she told Max. "What's on the schedule for today?"

"Let's go to the office and find out." Max gestured for her to follow him. "In any case, I'd like to talk over a few things with you before you get started."

Carole grimaced slightly as he turned away and headed down the aisle. What did Max want to talk to her about? Was he worried that she was going to get in trouble again now that she was back on the job? Fat chance—she would keep her grades up this time if she had to give up sleeping and eating to do it. There was no way she was ever going to risk being separated from the work she loved again.

As they entered the office, she noticed a phone message in her own handwriting tacked to the bulletin board over the desk. "Hey!" she said, pointing to it. "Did you ever call about those horses that woman wants to sell you?" She had taken the message a couple of days earlier when a local woman had called looking to place her two horses as schoolies. One of the horses sounded as though it had a few problems, but Carole was excited, as always, at the prospect of a new training challenge. She had been afraid that Max might not even consider taking the horses on—the woman claimed she would only let them go together.

"Yes, I spoke to Mrs. Rand once, but I've been so crazed that I haven't had a chance to call her back yet." Max ran a hand over his head and glanced at the battered black phone on the desk. "I was planning to see if I could go out there and see them tomorrow afternoon. I'm hoping the gelding isn't as poorly behaved as she's making him sound. It would be nice to have a couple of decent new horses right

15

around now—with all the new lesson kids and adult trail riders that have been coming out of the woodwork lately, we could really use them."

"Great!" Carole said excitedly, already thinking about the empty stalls and figuring out the best place to put a couple of newcomers. What could be better than starting the New Year with a pair of new horses? "And even if that gelding's not perfect right now, he's probably not beyond hope or anything. We could work with him until he's ready."

"Hmmm." Max sounded noncommittal. "Well, as I said, we'll just have to wait and see."

That gave Carole an idea. "When are you going?" she asked. "If it's before school starts up again next week, I could come along if you want."

"That would be great, as long as we get enough work done between now and then," Max replied. "It would be nice to have a second opinion. Of course, both of us can't leave if it's too busy. Otherwise Maureen and Ben will be run ragged."

Carole nodded quickly, pleased that Max seemed so eager for her opinion. It made her feel older and more mature than her seventeen years. "I understand. I know we're going to be extra busy this week with Red and Denise both out." Red O'Malley and Denise McCaskill, two of Pine Hollow's stable hands, had gotten married on New Year's Eve. They were away on a brief honeymoon in nearby Washington, D.C. "You can count on me."

"I know I can," Max said. "Of course, that doesn't mean I want to see you here at all hours of the day and night," he added sternly. "We don't want a repeat of—well, let's just say I don't want you overdoing things."

"Definitely not," Carole agreed hastily, realizing that the lecture portion of their talk had arrived. "I've learned my lesson, Max. I swear. You don't have to worry about my grades, or—or anything else."

She found herself blushing again, this time in shame. She wasn't sure she'd ever live down what she'd done when her grades had started slipping that fall. Her father, Max, and her friends had been shocked when they'd found out. Even now she found it hard to believe that she'd actually cheated on a test, peeked at the answers to keep her average from falling below a C, which was Max's minimum requirement for all school-age riders at Pine Hollow.

"I believe you," Max told her with a smile. "I believe you really have learned your lesson the hard way, and that you won't let anything like this happen again. Your good track record speaks for you."

Carole blushed. Max didn't pass out compliments often, which made them that much more meaningful when they came. "Thanks," she said simply.

Max glanced at the office clock and clapped his hands. "Okay, then. Let's get to work before the day's half over," he said briskly. He studied the chalkboard near the office door. "You can start by giving Patch his medicine and checking to see if the swelling's down on his sole. You and Maureen can start turning out horses when you're finished with that—Chip, Talisman, Memphis, and all the ponies are going out this morning, and someone needs to bring down more hay. After that . . ."

Carole grinned as Max rattled on, giving out his usual hundred-and-one-item to-do list. Yes, she was home.

TWO

Stevie Lake yawned as she wandered up the stable aisle toward her horse's stall. She had slept late that morning, doing her best to take advantage of her last few days of winter vacation.

"Glad you could make it, lazybones," Carole's familiar voice called teasingly.

Blinking, Stevie glanced over and realized that her friend was in an empty stall, sprinkling lime on a wet spot on the dirt floor. "Hey," she greeted her, stifling another yawn. "Hard at work already, I see."

Carole grimaced. "Yeah. And already wondering why I was so eager to get back to this."

Stevie laughed. Cleaning stalls wasn't anybody's idea of a good time, but she knew that Carole was kidding. Even if some tasks were less appealing than others, Carole had to be thrilled to be back doing what she loved best—taking care of horses. Ever since Stevie had known her, that was all Carole really wanted to do.

Stevie leaned against the wall, watching as her friend sprinkled more of the white powdery lime onto the stall floor. "Ah, the glorious smell of horse pee in the morning," she reflected. "What more could you wish for on your first day back?"

"How about a little help from a certain so-called best friend?" Carole suggested smilingly. "That is, unless you'd rather stand around and watch like some kind of lazy old pasture potato?"

Stevie opened her mouth to shoot back a retort but ended up shrugging instead. It was true. She did feel sort of lazy. "Hey, that's what vacation is for, right?" she said with a grin. "Hanging out. Being lazy. Doing nothing."

Carole tossed the scoop back in the lime bucket and cocked a dubious eye at Stevie. "For some people, maybe," she said, hoisting the bucket out of the way and setting about bedding down the stall. "But since when does Stevie Lake, the queen of energy, ever just hang out and do nothing? I thought you'd be here bright and early, sniffing around for another breaking story to cover for the school paper when you go back next week. Or maybe practicing dressage so you can kick Phil's butt at your next show."

Stevie sighed before she quite realized she was doing it. "Yeah," she said, glancing down the aisle at her horse, Belle, who had just stuck her head out over the half door of her stall. "Belle and I really should get back into some serious dressage training. Things have been so crazy lately, what with the holidays and everything, that it's been hard enough just to squeeze in a trail ride once in a while. At this point Belle probably doesn't even remember what a half-pass is."

Carole paused in her work, leaned on her pitchfork, and raised one eyebrow at Stevie. "You don't sound too thrilled about all this. Does this mean you're finally getting bored with dressage?"

Stevie grinned sheepishly. She knew that most people found it hard to believe that she was interested in a discipline requiring so much precision and restraint. *Precision* and *restraint* weren't the first words that leaped into anyone's head when Stevie's name came up, and she knew it. "No way," she said. "Not until Belle and I are at Prix St. Georges level at least." Her smile faded slightly. "It's just that right now, well, it sort of feels like we'll never get there. Like we're in a rut. Must be that postholiday letdown thing I'm always hearing about."

"Maybe," Carole said. "So why not plan something to look forward to? You could enter yourself in a dressage show sometime in the next month or two. That way you'd have something to work toward."

"Hmmm." Stevie toyed with the idea for a moment. Maybe Carole was right. Maybe all she needed was a goal—something to put the spark back in her riding. "I guess that could work."

"You don't sound too convinced." Carole smiled, letting herself out of the stall and resting her pitch-fork on the wheelbarrow in the aisle. "What happened to that killer competitive spirit we all know and—"

She was interrupted by the sound of someone clearing his throat. Glancing behind her, Stevie saw that George Wheeler was watching them over the half door of his horse's stall. She blinked in surprise. "Oh, hi, George," she said. "I didn't see you there."

"Sorry, I wasn't trying to eavesdrop," George said in his soft voice. "But I couldn't help hearing what you were saying, and I was just wondering something. Have you ever thought about going into eventing?"

"Eventing?" Stevie shrugged. She knew that George was an avid event rider. "I've ridden in a couple of one-day trials and stuff, back in Pony Club. But otherwise, I guess I haven't really thought about it much."

George let himself out of the stall, gently pushing his mare's nose back as she tried to follow. "I'm surprised you haven't thought about it more," he said. "I think you'd be really good at it. You're a really good all-around rider. And it would be another way to show off your dressage skills, along with your jumping skills, which everybody knows aren't too shabby either."

"Don't flatter her too much, George," Carole joked as she pushed the wheelbarrow down to the next occupied stall, where a chestnut gelding named Comanche was watching her curiously. "Her ego's big enough as it is."

Stevie ignored her friend's teasing. She was thinking about what George had said. "You know, you're right," she mused. "I wonder why I never saw it before. I mean, I love dressage—so that part's taken care of. And Belle's a good jumper and good at cross-country. . . . It could be a totally fun new thing for us to try!" The more she thought about it, the more excited she felt.

"Hmmm," Carole commented from Comanche's stall. "Actually, the only surprising thing about this idea is that you never thought of it before, Stevie. It's sort of a natural. You have a perfect personality for eventing. You're bold and aggressive, and you like to ride fast. . . ."

Stevie grinned. "I'll take that as a compliment," she said. "And you're right. This could be just the thing to get me and Belle out of our rut."

"Belle . . . ," Carole repeated. "What about Belle? Do you think she's up to it? I mean, I know she's great at dressage, but all that jumping . . ."

Stevie nodded slowly, glancing up the aisle at her

mare, who was still watching them. "I know she doesn't seem like the first choice of breeds for this sort of thing," she admitted. "But it's not like we're going to be trying out for the Olympics or anything. She'll be fine for, like pre-novice stuff or whatever. Right?" Suddenly realizing that George was still standing there, she looked at him for an opinion.

He was nodding. "I'll admit, I don't see too many Saddlebred-Arab crosses competing," he said. "But the jumps at the lower levels are pretty small, and Belle should be athletic enough."

"Cool." Stevie smiled, glad that George agreed with her own assessment. "I think we might need a little jumping practice before we hit the cross-country stuff, though. It's been a while."

"I could help you out with that if you want," George offered. "I mean, I know you could do fine by yourself. But Joyride was pretty green when I got her, so I've been through all the training before." He gestured at the tall gray mare in the stall behind him.

"That would be great!" Stevie said. She could hardly believe George was being so cool. Why had she thought he was such a nerd? "I could totally use all the help I can get."

They were discussing training strategy when Carole emerged from Comanche's stall a few minutes later. "Well, that was the last one," she announced, dropping her pitchfork on the full wheelbarrow. "I'd better get moving. But I should have a break in a little while. Want to go for a ride?" She glanced at Stevie.

"Sure," Stevie agreed, a little distracted. Her head was swimming with her new plans. How could she ever have thought the New Year was going to be dull? Turning herself and Belle into an event team was going to be a real challenge. And there was nothing Stevie liked more than a challenge. "Just come find me when you're ready."

Carole nodded and hurried off, pushing the wheelbarrow down the aisle toward the back exit. Stevie turned her attention back to George. She had a million and one questions for him. She couldn't wait to get started.

Lisa Atwood cut the engine of her car and just sat there for a moment, gazing at the grove of oak trees beyond Pine Hollow's small parking lot. Suddenly noticing that she was gripping the steering wheel, she smiled ruefully at herself.

Wow, she thought, relaxing her hands and rubbing them on her well-worn rust-colored breeches. *I guess Mom's really getting to me. It's a good thing I got out of the house when I did. If she gave me one more sympathetic look or murmured one more word about my "repression of deep-seated feelings of pain and rejection," I would have screamed.*

She thought about that for a minute or two until she started to get chilly. Finally, shaking off her thoughts, she climbed out of the car. Pocketing her keys, she started across the parking lot, gravel crunching under the hard soles of her paddock boots. Although she hadn't called Stevie or Carole before coming over, she hoped to find one or both of her best friends at Pine Hollow that day. She needed something familiar, physical, and real— something like a nice, long, relaxing trail ride—to help chase away the feeling of restlessness that seemed to be following her around for the past couple of days.

I guess it's that postholiday blah thing happening, she thought as she hurried toward the stable building. *Of course, this year I have a few more things to recover from than too much tinsel and fruitcake.*

She grimaced, realizing just how true that was. For the past year, Lisa had been dating Stevie's twin brother, Alex. They had been in love, and up until a couple of months earlier, Lisa had been certain that they were meant to be together forever. Then, somehow, things had changed. She and Alex had started spending more time arguing than being happy. He had grown insecure about their relationship, and she had gotten tired of constantly having to reassure him. Finally they had both realized they'd grown apart without really noticing, and on New Year's Eve they'd agreed to end their relationship.

By that point, the decision had been more of a relief than anything else. But as many times as Lisa tried to explain that to her mother, the message just didn't seem to be getting through.

"Don't hold back, darling," Mrs. Atwood had crooned after dinner the evening before, her voice dripping bitter sympathy. "I know exactly how you feel." Lisa had almost been able to read her mind at that point—she was sure her mother was thinking about the day Lisa's father had walked out after twenty-seven years of marriage. Mrs. Atwood still hadn't adjusted to the divorce, though she'd spent enough time and money trying. She still attended weekly group therapy meetings, better known as gripe therapy to Lisa and her friends. And now she seemed unable to understand that Lisa didn't feel a need to cry and moan and rehash every moment of her own breakup. After dealing with the idea of it for so long, she was pretty much resigned to it. A little sad, yes. A little uncertain about the future, certainly. But any twinge of regret or doubt or bitterness was behind her already.

Still, after hanging around with that bunch all this

time, I shouldn't be surprised if Mom can't conceive of someone moving on after a breakup, Lisa thought with another grimace as she reached the stable's wide double doors, which were shut against the January chill. *None of her gripe therapy pals seems to be capable of moving on from a hangnail, let alone a breakup. It's probably just as well that I didn't tell her about—*

"Scott!" she blurted out as she pushed open the door, almost banging it into the tall, good-looking guy standing just inside. Feeling a little flustered, she noticed that Scott Forester wasn't alone. "Um, I mean, hi, Scott and Callie. How's it going, you two?"

Scott and Callie both greeted her, but Lisa only seemed to be able to focus on Scott. "Hey, Lisa," he said, taking a step toward her. "What's up?"

"Thanks for the ride, Scott," Callie told her brother. "Don't bother to wait—I'll walk home when I'm done." Giving Lisa a quick wave, she hurried off in the direction of her horse's stall.

"That's my sister for you," Scott joked fondly. "There's no time for chitchat when there are horses to be ridden."

"I know just how she feels," Lisa replied with a smile. "Um, by the way, happy New Year."

"Ditto." Scott smiled tentatively. "So . . . um, how are you doing?"

His tone was carefully neutral, but Lisa guessed he was fishing for information. Everyone at Pine Hollow must have heard that she and Alex had broken up, and Scott had more than a passing interest in that particular topic. He and Lisa had been out on several dates during the weeks when she and Alex were experimenting with seeing other people. At first Lisa had been reluctant to get involved with him, even casually—it just seemed too awkward, since they shared most of the same friends. But after a certain point, she'd been forced to admit that there was a serious mutual attraction brewing between them. Even at that moment, standing in the dusty stable entryway, dressed in ratty old riding clothes, she could feel the sparks flying.

She blushed, hoping that Scott couldn't read her mind. "I'm okay," she said. "Great, actually."

"Really?" Scott looked hopeful but not completely convinced.

Lisa nodded firmly. "Really," she said. "The past is over. I'm ready to face the New Year—no regrets."

"Cool," Scott said with a broad smile. "Then how about if I take you to dinner tomorrow night to celebrate your New Year's perspective?"

Lisa gulped. She had mixed feelings about letting herself slide right into another relationship so soon. Still, looking up into Scott's guileless blue eyes, she

29

couldn't resist. "Sure," she said. "That sounds like fun."

"Great." Scott looked pleased. Before he could say anything else, Stevie appeared at the end of the stable aisle. Spotting Lisa, she called her name, sounding excited. Lisa couldn't help feeling a twinge of guilt—would Stevie feel awkward about finding her here with Scott? Even though it wasn't as if he was Alex's replacement, exactly, it might appear that way to Alex's twin sister.

But Stevie hardly seemed to take in the meaning of finding the two of them together as she rushed over, breathless and clutching a currycomb. "Sorry, Forester," she said bluntly. "You'll have to drool on Lisa some other time. I have big news for her right now."

"Really?" Lisa's worries, along with her slight annoyance at the interruption, were overtaken by curiosity. "What is it?"

Stevie grinned proudly. "I'm going to be an eventer!"

"Huh?" Lisa blinked.

Stevie rolled her eyes. "You know, eventing? As in combined training? I'm going to do that!"

"Oh." Lisa was still having a little trouble grasping Stevie's point. For one thing, Scott was standing so close it was kind of distracting. "Um, I know what eventing is. Why are you going to do it all of a sudden?"

"Come on. Let's grab Carole and go on a trail ride. I'll tell you all about it then." Stevie seized Lisa's arm and dragged her toward the aisle. Lisa hardly had time to wave good-bye to Scott before they left him behind.

THREE 3

"Almost ready," Callie murmured soothingly as she pulled her horse's forelock out from under the browband of his bridle. "Hope you don't mind working in the ring today, boy. It's a little cold to spend much time out on the trails."

Scooby merely blinked in response. Callie gave him a pat, then brought the reins over his head. Unhooking the stall guard, she led him out into the aisle. A flash of movement at the end of the aisle caught her eye, and she spun around quickly—only to see one of the stable cats batting at a fly. She sighed with relief, feeling foolish. She was really getting jumpy.

It hadn't been easy to drag herself to the stable. While one part of her was champing at the bit to get into serious training with her new horse, another part kept remembering all the unpleasant surprises she'd had to deal with lately, which were making her as spooky as a green-broke horse on a strange trail. Like the time a few days ago when she'd panicked at the sight of George's car pulling into the drive and had taken off into the woods as fast as Secretariat. Or that creepy incident with the face at the window the other night. And most of all, she kept reliving the day more than a week earlier, when she and Scooby had been deep in the state forest behind Pine Hollow. Alone. Or so she'd thought. . . .

"Come on," she said aloud to her horse, forcibly interrupting that line of thought. It wouldn't do her any good to dwell on all that. She'd gotten herself into this mess, and she was just going to have to face it down before it went any further. "The day's half over. We'd better get cracking."

She led Scooby down the aisle, planning to work on some schooling figures in the outdoor ring. Halfway to the entryway, she came upon Maureen Chance, who was emerging from a stall with a hoof pick in her hand.

"Hey," Maureen greeted her, giving Scooby a quick once-over. "Doing some training today?"

Callie winced, trying not to hear the unspoken *Finally!* in Maureen's sentence. She hadn't been spending nearly as much time at the stable lately as most new horse owners would, and she supposed she shouldn't be surprised that people had noticed. "Yeah," she replied. "I thought we'd work on some schooling figures in the outdoor ring. Is it free?"

"Far's I know," Maureen said with a shrug. "Lessons are over for today."

Callie nodded, clearing her throat nervously. "Er, so who else is around today?" she asked.

"What do you mean?" Maureen stuck her hoof pick in her jeans pocket and reached up with both hands to adjust her fiery ponytail.

"You know—like, people my age. Who all's here right now?" Callie asked. "Um, I was just wondering."

Maureen gave her a strange look, but answered. "I think I saw Stevie and what's-her-name, Lisa. Oh, and Carole and Ben are here, natch. And I just saw that studly brother of yours pulling out. A couple of the younger kids just got back from the trail. I guess that's about it."

"Oh. Okay. Thanks." Callie was already wishing she hadn't brought it up. Why would Maureen even notice if George was at the stable or not? Despite the fact that the new stable hand seemed to have radar when it came to spotting males of all shapes and sizes, George tended to blend into the woodwork no matter where he went.

Besides, who cares if he's here? she added rather defiantly. *I'm here to train, not to worry about George. Not anymore. I've wasted enough time on that already.*

Still, she couldn't resist speaking up again just as Maureen started to turn away. "Um, what about

George?" Callie asked. "George Wheeler. Is he around?"

Maureen smirked knowingly. "Ah, I should've guessed what you were after," she said. "Yeah, forgive me for leaving him out. I'm pretty sure he's still here. He took his mare out for a long hack this morning, and he's been puttering around the place ever since."

Callie was relieved to hear that George had already done his riding for the day, though she was also more than a little annoyed that Maureen seemed to think she had some kind of romantic interest in George. What was the deal with all those smirks and winks? Was it just Maureen's natural habit to look for scandal and intrigue everywhere? Or had George said something to make her think there was something going on?

She did her best to put that out of her mind. The last thing she wanted to do was press Maureen for information—that would only encourage her to keep thinking what she was thinking. *Besides,* Callie thought as she tugged gently at Scooby's reins to get him moving again, *the sooner I get out into the ring, the less likely it is that George will turn up suddenly and want to chat.*

Soon she and Scooby emerged from the stable aisle. Pausing just long enough to fasten the chin strap of her hard hat, Callie mounted in the high-ceilinged entryway. After adjusting her stirrups and double-checking her girth, she squeezed Scooby with her calves and aimed him toward the open side of the wide double doors.

"Hey! Callie!" a young voice called from somewhere behind her. "Don't forget to touch it."

Callie pulled up and glanced over her shoulder. A girl named May Grover from the intermediate riding class was standing near the stable aisle, staring at her with concern. "What?" Callie said blankly.

"The lucky horseshoe," May said, her tone indicating that Callie might be just slightly stupid. "You didn't touch it."

"Oh," Callie said. Like most stables, Pine Hollow had a long list of traditions. Callie had only been riding there for a little over six months, so it was sometimes hard to keep track of them all. She turned Scooby in a tight circle so that they could come around again beside the misshapen old iron horseshoe nailed to the wall beside the main entrance. As she understood it, the hunk of metal was afforded magical properties by most of Pine Hollow's riders, who swore that no one had ever been seriously injured while riding after touching it.

After brushing the horseshoe with the tips of her gloved fingers, Callie headed for the door once again. Minutes later she had Scooby walking around the schooling ring on a loose rein. Doing her best to push all distractions out of her mind, she focused on the coming session, planning her strategy. Scooby was in pretty good condition already, but he needed plenty of schooling and conditioning before they would be ready to tackle their first endurance race. Callie had already come up with a series of exercises designed to improve Scooby's balance, suppleness, and responsiveness, and she spent her warm-up time running through her plans once again. Then, when Scooby was ready, they got started.

A few minutes later Callie was concentrating on a double-loop gymnastics exercise when she became aware of hoofbeats approaching. *Darn,* she thought. *So much for having the ring to myself today. I knew this was too good to be true.*

She glanced up to see who was coming, praying it wasn't one of the intermediate riders wanting to set up a jump course or a beginner who wouldn't be able to keep her horse from running up behind Scooby or otherwise getting in Callie's way. But the person she saw fit neither category.

"Hi, Callie!" George called cheerfully, waving to her from aboard Joyride. "Mind if I join you?"

What? Callie thought. Her mind froze, unwilling to accept this new wrinkle. *What in the world is he doing here? Maureen said he already took Joy out for a long time today. So why would he want to work her again now?*

It didn't make sense. Still, she supposed she shouldn't be so shocked. Nothing George had done lately made much sense—from accidentally-on-purpose loosening her horse's shoe out on the trail to peeking in her living room window late at night.

She stared openmouthed at George, who didn't seem to be waiting for an answer to his own question. Steering Joyride alongside the gate, he expertly leaned down and opened it without dismounting. Seconds later he was in the ring with Callie, riding toward her at a brisk walk.

Joyride, a fairly high-strung Trakehner, snorted and pinned her ears suspiciously as she approached Scooby, but George didn't seem to notice. "Hi there!" he said cheerfully, bringing his horse to a stop just a few steps away. "What are you doing? Giving ol' Scoob a little workout?"

"Um, yeah." Callie nudged Scooby to get him to step away. The gelding obeyed, though his ears flicked back and forth nervously as he picked up on his rider's discomfort. Callie was trying her hardest to keep her fear from taking over—the fear that was becoming increasingly common whenever George turned up and did something weird and unpredictable. Like tracking her down deep in the state forest, miles from anywhere. Or showing up in the ring now, when he was supposed to be finished riding for the day. "We were just doing some figures and stuff."

"Cool." George smiled blandly, completely unaware of her consternation. Or at least acting as though he was.

Feeling tense, Callie decided it was time to take action. "Well, we'd better get back to work," she said, gathering her reins. Picking up on her nervousness, Scooby tossed his head, but he moved forward at a trot.

A moment later Joyride caught up to the Appaloosa gelding, trotting briskly along at his inside. Callie glanced over to see George grinning at her as he kept hold of the mare's naturally long stride, keeping it carefully matched to Scooby's.

"Hope you don't mind," he said. "Joy could use a good session in the arena right about now. Maybe we could just work along with you and Scooby for a while."

Callie was trying to come up with a response to that when she spotted Stevie emerging from the stable building, leading her tacked-up horse. Carole was right behind her with Starlight, and a second later Lisa joined them, leading a school horse named Barq.

"Guys!" Callie called, hoping her voice didn't sound quite as desperate as she thought it did. "Hey, you guys! Over here!"

The trio glanced in her direction and waved. Peeking at George out of the corner of her eye, Callie gave a quick kick to send Scooby rushing toward the gate. Outside, Stevie mounted smoothly and rode toward the ring. "Hey, Callie," she called cheerily. "What are you—"

"I'm ready!" Callie shouted, doing her best to drown out the rest of Stevie's question. "Should we go ahead and hit the trail now?" She widened her eyes meaningfully at Stevie, rolling them slightly backward and hoping her friend would pick up on the message.

Stevie didn't miss a beat. "Great," she said. "Sorry we kept you waiting, Callie. But we can get going now."

Callie smiled with relief. Quickly leaning over to open the gate, she let herself out. As she turned her horse to close the gate again, she saw George riding toward them, looking confused.

"Are you all going on a trail ride?" he asked.

"Uh-huh." Lisa had joined them by now, though Carole was still back near the stable entrance, fiddling with Starlight's girth. "We thought we'd ride out to the creek or somewhere."

"That sounds fun," George said. He hesitated, then gave Stevie and Lisa a tentative smile. "You know, I was going to work in the ring this afternoon. But a trail ride sounds kind of relaxing."

Blinking at Stevie, he added, "And I was hoping we'd have a chance to talk more about your eventing plans."

Callie had no idea what that last comment was all about, but to her amazement and dismay, she saw that Stevie looked torn. Was she actually thinking about letting George invite himself along? "Sorry," she blurted out quickly. "It'll have to wait, George. This is strictly a girls' day out. I'm sure you understand."

Without waiting for an answer, she urged Scooby forward, aiming him toward the trails. Soon he was moving at a brisk trot. She could only pray that her friends would take their cue from her once again and follow before George could figure out a way to butt in anyway.

Hearing hoofbeats behind her, she heaved a sigh of relief. Then she had a sudden vision of Stevie, Carole, and Lisa standing back at the stable, gaping stupidly as George trotted after her, and she twisted around so fast that she nearly unbalanced herself. To her renewed relief, she saw Stevie and Lisa trotting along just behind her. Carole was still a little way behind, but Starlight's fast, swinging trot was closing the gap. George was still in the ring, though he'd dismounted and was staring after them as Joyride nosed at some weeds beneath the fence.

Callie slowed her horse to a walk, knowing that

her friends' horses weren't warmed up yet. Soon they were riding four abreast across the broad, frost-bitten pasture that stood between the stable yard and the woods.

"Hey, Callie," Carole said, "I didn't know you were coming with us today."

"Neither did I," Callie replied grimly, willing herself not to look back and check on what George was doing. "It was sort of a last-minute change of plans."

She didn't explain further, though she was sure her friends were curious. Somehow, she couldn't bring herself to get into the whole story just then.

"Well, we're glad you could come along," Stevie said carefully. "Um, but do you think that George wanted to—"

"I'm sick of George Wheeler!" Callie snapped before her friend could finish her sentence. "If I had to spend a whole trail ride with him, I'd probably puke."

Her friends were silent for a long moment. Then Carole changed the subject, saying something about Starlight's hooves. Callie kept her eyes trained straight ahead, between Scooby's pricked ears. She realized that her friends might think she was acting like a jerk, but she didn't care. They weren't the ones who had to deal with George every time they turned around. They weren't the ones who spent every day kicking themselves for ever letting him into their lives. They couldn't possibly understand what that was like. So they could simply think whatever they wanted to think. Callie was just glad she'd escaped this time.

Half an hour later Lisa swayed gently with the motion of Barq's walk, not even trying to maintain a proper riding position. Instead she slumped into the saddle, letting the Arabian gelding follow Starlight, who was just ahead of them on the wooded trail.

Though her body was out on the trail with her friends, her thoughts were back at the stable. Brooding over her latest encounter with Scott, she wondered whether she should have agreed to go out with him again.

I'm free now, she reminded herself. *Independent. I should be thinking about what went wrong with Alex, trying to figure out what I want out of life—not just flinging myself at the next cute guy who smiles at me. Right?*

She couldn't quite feel sorry that she'd made that date with Scott, though. In fact, she was looking forward to it. Of course, that didn't mean she didn't have doubts about hooking up with him so soon. Were the feelings she had for him real? Or did it help, at least a little, that he was so handsome and attentive and eager to be with her—exactly when she was feeling a little insecure about life and love and the future?

That reminded her of her mother. Lisa knew that part of the reason her mother couldn't believe she wasn't devastated about breaking up with Alex was that she couldn't understand how any woman could be better off without a man in her life.

But I'm not like that, Lisa told herself. *Am I?*

"Lisa? Lisa! Yo, Lisa!"

Blinking, Lisa glanced over her shoulder, realizing that Stevie was calling her name. "Huh?" she said blankly, suddenly remembering where she was.

"I said, are you okay?" Stevie said. "Barq looks like he's trying to take a bite out of Starlight's tail."

"Oops." Lisa blinked and looked at her horse's head, realizing that he had run up on Starlight so that his nose was almost touching the other horse's rump. Feeling sheepish, she gathered her reins and sat up straight, half-halting until her horse backed off. "Sorry about that, Carole."

"S'okay," Carole replied, glancing over her shoulder. "You know Starlight couldn't care less. But it's not like you to let Barq get away with that kind of stuff."

"I know. Sorry," Lisa said, leaning forward to pat her horse on the neck. "I guess I'm a little distracted today."

"Oh yeah?" Stevie sounded interested. "How come?"

"Um, I was just thinking about, you know, stuff." Lisa hesitated, not sure whether she should go into more detail. Her gaze rested briefly on Callie, riding along in front of Carole. It was still a little weird having her along as part of their group. Lisa and Stevie and Carole had been a threesome for so long that it always felt kind of strange to hang out with other people. Plus, Callie was Scott's sister. But that wasn't what was really holding Lisa back. She was still worried about how her feelings would affect Stevie. Would Stevie think she was being disloyal to Alex by even thinking about moving on so soon after their breakup? Stevie and Alex sometimes seemed to get along about as well as cats and dogs, but Lisa knew that beneath all the jokes and arguments, the twins were fiercely loyal to each other.

Still, Lisa couldn't resist the urge to share her feelings. She had relied on her friends' input in her life for too long to start holding back now. She felt a little awkward about mentioning Scott in front of Callie, but she figured she could leave that part out for now.

"It's just, um, Mom has really been on my case for the past couple of days," she admitted. "You know, because of the breakup. She seems to think I should be a big puddle of rejection and self-hatred or something. Since I'm not, I guess she thinks I'm covering up my true feelings. You know, repression or compensation or whatever."

"Hmmm," Stevie said, pulling Belle up beside Barq as the trail widened. "Sounds like ol' Eleanor has been spending too much time with the gripers again."

Lisa was glad to see that Stevie's expression was sympathetic and concerned, but not upset or angry. Carole, on the other hand, was visibly disturbed as she glanced at Lisa over her shoulder. "Carole?" Lisa said, surprised. "What's the matter?"

Without further ado, Carole burst into tears. She managed to bring Starlight to a halt, then dropped her reins on his withers and buried her face in her hands. The others pulled up, too. Lisa and Stevie exchanged confused and worried glances. Callie just looked startled as she circled Scooby around and walked him back toward the others.

"Carole?" Stevie said, nudging Belle over beside Starlight. "What's wrong?"

Suddenly Lisa realized she hadn't really talked to Carole in a couple of days—not since New Year's Eve, when Carole and her new boyfriend Cam had had their first fight. At least that was what Lisa had heard from other people. Feeling a little guilty about being so self-absorbed, she smiled at Carole sympathetically. "Does this mean you and Cam haven't made up yet?" she asked. "I heard you guys had a fight on New Year's Eve."

"N-not exactly," Carole managed to say between sobs. She wiped her eyes and glanced at her friends, her face miserable. "I mean, we didn't just have a fight. He dumped me."

"Oh." Lisa tried not to sound as skeptical as she felt. She still remembered how devastating that kind of situation could be. At the beginning of a relationship, every little argument and disagreement felt like the end of the world. "Um, have you guys tried talking about it? I mean—"

"Yeah," Stevie interjected, loosening her reins as Belle lowered her head and sniffed at the brownish weeds beside the trail. "Sometimes things get blown out of proportion, especially when you're just starting out. Cam really loves you. He'll want to—"

"He doesn't," Carole interrupted, more tears spilling out of her wide brown eyes. "He made that pretty clear. All he cared about was . . . was . . ." She sobbed again.

"What?" Lisa couldn't imagine what this was about, though she was starting to think it might be more serious than the typical petty first tiff. Carole was pretty sensitive, but she wasn't the melodramatic type. She glanced at the others. Stevie looked just as confused and concerned as Lisa felt. Callie, who had been quiet until then, was gazing at Carole worriedly. "Carole, you can tell us," Lisa added, dropping her stirrups to stretch her legs as Barq stood quietly with the other horses. "What happened?"

"Remember our gift exchange?" Carole asked.

Lisa shrugged. "Sure," she said, and Stevie nodded. Carole had spent more than a week shopping and planning, trying to figure out the perfect Christmas gift for Cam.

"Well, as it turned out, there was only one gift Cam really wanted from me," Carole said, her voice sad and bitter. "One very, um, intimate kind of gift. If you know what I mean."

Lisa's eyes widened. "Oh!" she said, wondering if she was misunderstanding. "You mean—"

"Uh-huh." Carole gulped back another sob. "He made it quite clear. That's why he brought me to the hayloft on New Year's Eve. He thought it would be the perfect spot, nice and private. And when I wouldn't go along with it, when I told him I wasn't ready for that yet, he told me it was over."

"That rat!" Stevie exclaimed so angrily that Belle flinched beneath her. "That total jerk! I can't believe he'd do that! What a total, complete, utter . . . ," she sputtered, clearly too furious to settle on just the right descriptive name.

Callie was shaking her head. "Wow," she said. "Sounds like quite a piece of work."

Lisa was too shocked to speak for a moment. She and Carole and Stevie had all known Cam in junior high, and back then he had been a really nice guy. It was hard to believe that someone could change so much in a few years. But if what Carole was saying was true—and looking at her tearstained face, Lisa was convinced that it was—then that was just what had happened. Nice, polite, caring Cam had morphed into a selfish, manipulative cad.

Stevie was still muttering angrily, but Lisa just felt sad. "I know this has got to be rough, Carole," she said, wondering why her friend seemed to have such bad luck with guys. "But try not to beat yourself up about it. He fooled all of us."

"Yeah," Stevie added, scratching Belle on the withers to soothe her. "I've seen players before, but Cam is obviously a real pro. You can do way better than him."

Lisa was expecting Carole to argue—she'd been so smitten with Cam that it had seemed she'd forgotten other guys existed—but instead she just nodded thoughtfully. "Uh-huh," she murmured. "I guess you're right."

"You're right I'm right," Stevie said firmly. "You deserve someone who cares about you—someone who'll treat you right, without pressuring you or playing games."

"I'm sorry for whining on about Mom and Alex before," Lisa said, still feeling a little guilty for neglecting her friend in her hour of need, even unintentionally. "I guess I was so wrapped up in my own problems that I didn't even realize what you were going through."

"Don't worry about it," Carole reassured her. She smiled wanly through her tears. "I—I was trying not to let it show. And what with starting back to work and everything, I thought I was pulling it off for a while there. I guess it's that repression stuff your mom was talking about, huh?" She giggled, then hiccuped.

"Hey, repression is cool," Callie put in with a smile. "But you know what I discovered is the only real cure for this kind of thing?"

"Bloody, violent revenge?" Stevie suggested hopefully.

Callie laughed. "Nope," she said. "A nice long canter. How about it?"

Carole's smile looked more sincere this time. "That could work," she said. "Why don't we give it a try?"

"Sounds good," Lisa agreed, shooting Callie a grateful glance. They would have plenty of time to talk about this in the days and weeks to come, as

Carole's heart slowly healed. But at the moment, Callie was right. The best thing for Carole would be to take her mind off it for a while by doing something she loved.

"So what are we waiting for?" Stevie glanced at the wide, smooth trail ahead of them. They had followed it many times over the years, and they all knew that it emerged at a broad, gently sloping field. It was the perfect spot for a canter.

Lisa gathered her reins. "Come on," she said, suddenly feeling happy in spite of everything. "Let's go!"

FOUR

"So, Stevie," Phil Marsten said as Stevie pulled her car neatly into an empty spot in Pine Hollow's parking area the next day. "I have a question for you."

"Huh?" Stevie blinked, momentarily distracted from the plans and ideas that had been tumbling through her head during the ride over to the stable from Phil's house. She glanced at her boyfriend. "What is it?"

Phil grinned. "Are you ever going to talk about anything except eventing ever again?" he asked. "I mean, it's not that I'm not enjoying this monologue—er, I mean, conversation. I'm just wondering."

Stevie stuck out her tongue at him as she pulled the key out of the ignition. "Very funny," she said, knowing that he was teasing her. She and Phil had met years earlier at a summer riding camp, and they'd been inseparable ever since. Their relationship had gone through a few ups and downs over the years, but their strong underlying friendship had carried them through, along with their shared sense of humor. "Come on, let's go, before the little kids grab all the best horses and you end up riding fat old Patch on our trail ride."

The two of them climbed out of the car and headed for the stable. As they entered, Stevie started talking about her plans again. "I really don't know why I never thought to try it before." She was excited just thinking about the new world that was opening up before her. "I mean, it totally makes sense. I love dressage. I love jumping. What could be better?" Remembering Phil's comment, she grinned. "Oh, and by the way—eventing, eventing, eventing!"

Phil let out a mock groan and pretended to wing his hard hat at her head, though in actuality he merely tossed it gently in her direction. Stevie caught it easily and tucked it under her arm, still smiling.

Ben Marlow was crossing the entryway with a broom in his hand when Stevie and Phil entered. Stevie shot the stable hand a quick smile, expecting him to ignore her and hurry on his way, as usual. She was already turning back toward Phil to say something else about her eventing plans when she heard Ben clear his throat.

"Er, hello," he said gruffly.

Stevie blinked in surprise. Glancing at Ben again, she saw that he was looking at her, his expression a shade less hostile than usual. "Oh," she said. "Um, hi. How's it going, Ben?"

Beside her, Phil nodded to the other guy. "Hey," he said.

Ben gave a weird little half shrug and glanced at the door. "Pretty cold out there, huh?" he muttered. Before either of the others could answer, he cleared his throat again and then hurried off, disappearing down the stable aisle.

Stevie blinked. Was she imagining things, or had Ben Marlow just commented on the weather? Phil looked surprised, too.

"That was bizarre," Stevie said as soon as she was sure Ben was out of earshot. "Since when did Monosyllabic Marlow turn into Mr. Small Talk?"

Phil shrugged. "Maybe he has a crush on you," he joked.

"Yeah, right." Stevie snorted, brushing a strand of dark blond hair out of her eyes. "Trust me, if there's anyone he's hot for around here, it's not me."

"Does that mean you still think he's after Carole?" Phil asked. "I thought he blew her off after they kissed that time."

"Yeah." Stevie wrinkled her nose, staring off in the direction Ben had gone. "Still, the way he looks at her sometimes . . . I don't know. I guess they're just friends, like Carole says. He's weird, that's all. Antisocial." She shook her head. "I sort of wish he'd stay away from her for a while, especially after what she's just been through with Cam. She doesn't need to deal with more head games right now."

Phil shrugged again. "Well, they do work together, so I—"

"Hey, good-looking," a voice drawled, interrupting him.

Stevie turned and saw Maureen emerging from the hallway leading to the office and tack room. She rolled her eyes, guessing that the stable hand's compliment hadn't been directed at her. Sure enough, Maureen was grinning at Phil as she eyed him up and down, from his slightly tousled brown hair to his well-worn paddock boots. Stevie sighed. From the first day she'd arrived at Pine Hollow, Maureen had made a point of flirting with every guy she encountered, from Red O'Malley to Scott Forester to the hay delivery man. Just about the only one who seemed to be safe from her attention was Max, probably because he was her boss.

Maureen had better watch out, she thought. *This boy-crazy act of hers isn't going to make her too popular around here. Especially if she keeps making eyes at other people's boyfriends.*

Stevie knew she didn't have to worry about

Phil—he wasn't about to be swayed by Maureen's long legs and cool gold-flecked eyes. But some girl-friends might not be quite so confident. Besides, worried or not, Stevie couldn't help feeling a little annoyed that Maureen would flirt so blatantly right in front of her.

She was tempted to say something to Maureen about the way she was acting, but she bit her tongue as the phone rang from the direction of the office and the stable hand turned and hurried off to answer it. Stevie sighed again. Maybe she would talk to Maureen one of these days. But not right then.

"Heads up," she called to Phil, tossing him his hard hat. He caught it easily, swishing it onto his head in one smooth motion. Stevie grinned, re-membering how she'd taught him that trick years earlier. Forgetting all about Maureen and Ben and everything else, she was suddenly eager to get outside and ride with her boyfriend. "Come on, let's hit the tack room!"

"Large, small, large, large, pony," Carole mut-tered, quickly hanging the newly cleaned nylon girths slung over her arm on the proper pegs on the tack room wall. "Small, pony, large . . ." As soon as she finished her task, she was supposed to meet Max next door in the office to go look at the potential new school horses. "Small, small, large . . ."

56

"Carole?" a low, tentative voice said from behind her, so close that she jumped in surprise, almost dropping the rest of the girths.

She spun around. "Ben?" she said. "Oh! You startled me."

"Sorry." Ben took a step backward, looking strangely anxious. "Uh, I wanted to, you know, talk to you. About something."

Carole gulped, scanning the past couple of hours in her mind. Ben looked so weird, she was suddenly convinced that she must have done something horribly wrong, like put antiseptic in the fly-spray bottles or left the front pasture gate open. "What is it?" she asked worriedly. "What's wrong?"

"What? Oh, um, nothing." Ben cleared his throat. "I just—It's Firefly."

"What about her?" Firefly was a young mare Max had bought the previous summer. Carole and Ben had been working together on her training before Carole's grounding. "Has she been making progress since, um—you know?" She blushed slightly, still feeling ashamed when she thought about her long absence.

Ben nodded. "She's good," he said. "Uh, but the clippers—well. She still hates them. More than most."

"Ah." Carole thought about that. Firefly was pretty high-strung, and her ground training had needed plenty of work when she'd first arrived. Carole and Ben had managed to bring her along on most of the basics—the mare would now lead, tie, load, and stand quietly for grooming, bathing, and tacking. But she'd always been antsy when she heard the electric clippers turn on, and now it sounded as though Ben hadn't worked through that with her yet. That was surprising. Ben was one of the most patient people Carole had ever met when it came to training horses, and with most horses he could easily have solved such a simple issue long ago. "Well, let's see," she said. "Maybe it's time to approach the clippers thing in a different way. . . ."

She and Ben discussed the problem for a minute or two. Ben told her what he'd been trying so far, then Carole gave him all the ideas she could come up with.

"I'm going with Max to look at those new horses today," she told him. "But I could help you with her over the weekend if you want."

"Thanks." Ben coughed and glanced at her, then at the floor. "You—You really know your stuff."

Carole was astounded. She'd assumed that Ben respected her horse-related knowledge and experience, as she did his. But she'd never imagined him coming right out and saying it like that.

Before she could think of a response, Maureen stuck her head into the room. "Yo, Hanson," she said, spotting Carole. "Heads up, girl. Max is looking for you."

"What? Oh, thanks," Carole said, distracted. She still wanted to say something to Ben, to acknowledge what he'd said somehow, but he was already slipping out of the room past Maureen. Carole sighed, then turned toward the office door. Max was waiting. She would just have to figure out Ben Marlow later.

Despite that vow, she spent most of the short ride over to Mrs. Rand's farm pondering the possible meanings of the encounter in the tack room. She only snapped out of her reverie when Max hit the turn signal, pulling off the road into a gravel driveway. "Are we here?" Carole asked, glancing around curiously. "Wow. Nice place."

"Uh-huh." Max pulled slowly up the drive, heading toward a small green barn to one side of the Federal-style brick house. As he turned and pulled into a parking spot beside an ancient pickup truck, Carole spotted a medium-sized light gray pony trotting around the paddock. The little gelding was snorting and tossing his head, which made his flowing white mane dance over his beautifully crested neck.

Carole let out a low whistle. "Check out that gorgeous pony," she said excitedly. "He looks like he's at least part Welsh, don't you think? I wonder if that's one of the horses Mrs. Rand wants to sell?"

Max shrugged. "Looks like there are only two horses out here," he commented, gesturing toward the fence near the barn, where another horse was tied.

Carole glanced at the second horse, a bay mare, probably about sixteen hands, with two white socks and a large, plain head. She was standing calmly at the fence, her eyes half closed.

"She looks nice," she commented, taking in the mare's stout build and strong hindquarters. "Burly, too. If she's as calm and well-trained as Mrs. Rand claimed, she'd be perfect for adult beginners."

"We'll see," Max said simply. But he, too, was watching the mare with interest.

Carole's gaze soon wandered back to the pony. She got out of the car and strolled toward the paddock fence as Max walked over to the house. The pony watched her suspiciously, standing stock-still in the middle of the paddock. Carole leaned on the fence and clucked softly. The pony snorted. After a moment's hesitation, he walked toward her, his soft dark eyes curious.

"It's okay, little boy," Carole crooned, staying as still as possible. "I just want to say hi. You are a flashy fellow, aren't you?" She ran her eyes admiringly over the pony's body, which was practically flawless. Though the gelding was wearing his shaggy winter coat and was rumpled and dusty from rolling around in the paddock, Carole could easily picture him clipped and braided, circling a hunter course at an A circuit show.

As Carole continued to talk softly to the pony, he came closer. Before long he was snuffling at her palm, a curious expression in his dark eyes.

"That's right," Carole murmured, reaching around carefully to stroke his neck. The pony stood still, though she could feel him trembling slightly. "Good boy. What a nice boy." She smiled. There was something about the pony she really liked, and it wasn't his good looks. He had a light in his eyes, a spark of intelligence and energy that appealed to her.

I hope Max likes him, she thought, scratching the pony's crest. He was finally starting to relax, his ears flopping as he enjoyed her attention. *It would be fun to have this guy at Pine Hollow. With a little work— well, okay, maybe more than a little—I bet he'd be able to take some of the smaller intermediates to some good shows.*

Suddenly the pony tossed his head and jumped away, staring at something over Carole's right shoulder. Glancing behind her, Carole saw that Max was returning, accompanied by a wizened little woman wrapped in an enormous wool coat and a bright red scarf. Carole assumed that the woman was Mrs. Rand, the horses' elderly owner.

". . . and I just want to be sure I understand," Max was saying as the two adults reached Carole. "You want to sell these horses, but only to someone who will take them both?"

"That's right." Mrs. Rand pulled her scarf more tightly around the loose, papery skin of her throat. "These two have been together for years. Jinx— that's the little one there—is very attached to Maddie, and vice versa. I couldn't bear to separate them now."

"I see." Max's voice was neutral, though Carole could guess what he was thinking.

He probably figures the real reason she wants them to go together is she knows that's the only way she'll get anyone to take the pony, she thought, her earlier optimistic thoughts evaporating as she watched Max stare critically at the pony, who was now cantering erratically around the paddock, tossing his head and letting out a little buck every few strides. *Anyone other than the meat buyers at an auction, that is.*

She bit her lip as Jinx continued to jump around. Despite his good looks and appealing expression, Carole had to admit that his behavior didn't exactly scream "lesson horse." At his size, most adults and older teenagers were too tall and heavy to ride him comfortably. And until he learned some manners, he just wouldn't be safe for most younger kids to handle or ride. It would take a lot of work, skill, and patience to turn him into anything resembling a safe child's mount, and even so, he might never be a beginner's pony.

Maybe he'll calm down under saddle, she thought hopefully. *Maybe he's just not used to having strange people around. I'm sure he'd adjust soon enough to that, though.*

Max quickly introduced Carole to Mrs. Rand, who nodded politely, then turned to gesture at the mare. "That's the other horse right there," the woman said. "Madison has been with me a long time. But she was a fine show horse in her younger days. Did the jumpers."

Carole was just turning her attention to the bay mare when a short, lithe man with bushy dark eyebrows and quick, lively brown eyes emerged from the barn and hurried toward them. "Ah, Stanley, there you are," Mrs. Rand said, waving him over with one gloved hand. "This is my hired man, Stanley," she told Max and Carole. "He'll be showing you the horses."

"Call me Stan," the farmhand said with a smile, tipping his battered cowboy hat. Stepping forward, he shook hands first with Max and then with Carole. His grip was firm and his hand felt strong and callused.

"All right, then," Mrs. Rand said. "If you'll excuse me, this cold goes right through my old bones.

Stanley should be able to answer any questions you have about the horses, but I'll be inside if you need me."

"Thank you, Mrs. Rand," Max said as the elderly woman turned and headed back toward the warmth of the big brick house.

As soon as she was gone, Max smiled at Stan. "Okay," he said. "Should we start with the mare?"

"All right," Stan said agreeably. "Her name's Madison—Maddie—and she's good as gold. The three esses, as my daddy used to say: sensible, sound, and safe." Stan walked toward the mare, clucking softly to wake her up. Maddie flicked her ears at him and greeted him with a soft snort. "The tack's over there on the fence," Stan called to Max and Carole. "You can help get her ready if you want."

Max nodded approvingly. "Thanks. We will," he said, shooting Carole a look.

Carole didn't have to be told twice. She was as eager as Max was to see if this mare was really as nice as she seemed. Finding out how her ground manners were would give them a good idea about how she would fit in at Pine Hollow, where she'd be handled by all sorts of riders.

The mare gave them no trouble at all, barely swishing her tail as they tightened the girth and accepting the bit easily. When she was ready, Stan led her to the gate of a second paddock across the path from the one where Jinx was still trotting around excitedly. The mare waited patiently while Stan swung the gate open, then followed him through.

"I'll give her a whirl first," Stan said, checking the girth and then mounting in one smooth motion. Maddie stood like a rock as the farmhand fiddled with the stirrups. At his signal, she stepped off willingly.

Carole watched critically as Stan put the mare through her paces. He walked her, turning her left and right and riding in a circle. Then he moved to a trot and a canter, demonstrating both leads, which Maddie picked up easily. After that he aimed her at a makeshift jump set up in the middle of the paddock, which the mare cleared easily and without hesitation.

"She looks good," Max said casually when Stan pulled up in front of them. "Mind if I give her a go?"

"Be my guest." Stan dismounted, and Max swung aboard.

Carole smiled as she watched him. Max was so busy running Pine Hollow—looking after the horses, teaching lessons, and taking care of the business end of things—that she rarely saw him in the saddle. Whenever she did, she was always a little startled by how good he was. The mare responded just as nicely to him as she had to Stan, and Carole could tell by Max's expression that he liked her a lot.

After a few minutes, Max rode Maddie back to the gate and dismounted. "Nice," he said, giving her a pat. "Very well trained." He pursed his lips, glancing at the pony across the way. Jinx was at the fence watching them, his small ears pricked in their direction. As Max led Maddie out through the gate, the pony suddenly snorted, whirled, and kicked up his heels before racing across the paddock. "I suppose we'd better take a look at the other one now," Max added.

This time Stan didn't suggest that they help tack up. "You might want to stand back," he said instead. "Last time I tightened his girth, he about took my head off."

The next ten minutes were a real battle. Jinx fought Stan every step of the way, dodging aside so that the saddle pad slipped off, bucking to try to throw off the saddle, letting out a quick cow kick when Stan tightened the girth, and cementing his mouth closed at first sight of the bridle. Stan was patient but firm, insisting that the pony accept the tack, and won out in the end each time.

"Looks like his ground manners are a little rusty," Max commented blandly when Stan finally had the pony tacked and ready.

Stan sighed. "Jinx here is quite a handful, I won't

66

lie to you. I only wish I had time to work with him. Unfortunately, taking care of this place keeps me too busy for that sort of thing. He's got a good heart, but as for his training . . . well, let's just say there are a few holes."

Craters, more like, Carole thought ruefully, thinking of the way the pony had bucked at the weight of the saddle. *I bet he's never had any professional training at all. He just doesn't know any better.*

Stan checked the girth once more, earning a nasty look from the pony. "I'm a little big for him, but he's stronger than he looks." He was still a little breathless from wrestling with the girth. He grinned. "Here goes nothing." The farmhand swung into the saddle—not an easy task, since Jinx jumped to one side and started trotting forward as soon as he felt the man's weight on the stirrup. But somehow he managed to get up there, and with some visible effort he soon had the pony moving around the paddock at a choppy walk. After a moment, Jinx gave in and lowered his head, walking smoothly and swinging into a graceful trot at Stan's signal.

"Nice gaits," Carole said hopefully, glancing at Max.

Max never took his eyes off the pony, which had suddenly spotted Madison standing at the fence. Jinx seemed to take this as his cue to let off a quick buck. It was a mild one, and Stan sat it out easily. But he pulled up in front of them a moment later, sweating despite the cold weather.

"There you go," he said simply. "Mrs. Rand wanted me to show him to you, so that's what I've done. Up to you if you want to give him a whirl yourself."

Max pursed his lips uncertainly, glancing from Jinx to Madison and back again. Carole guessed that he was searching for a polite way to say thanks but no thanks. She also guessed that he was wishing there was some way to have Madison, who seemed in every way the perfect school horse. Carole bit her lip, glancing at Jinx.

"I'll give him a shot," she offered quickly. "Just let me run and get my hard hat out of the car."

Max looked dubious. "Are you sure?" he asked. "I mean, I'm sure you can handle him, Carole, but . . ."

Carole could tell that he thought riding the pony was a waste of time, and he was probably worried about her safety. "Don't worry," she said, turning toward the car. "Back in a sec."

When she returned, Max was still looking uncertain. "I don't know if this is a good idea, Carole," he said as she strapped on her helmet. "I want you to be careful, okay? Hop off if he starts acting up too much—don't take any chances."

Stan nodded. "At least you're closer to the right size for him," he told Carole. "Maybe he'll like that better. I'll hold him for you if you want to adjust the stirrups from the ground. It can be tough to get him to hold still long enough to do it once you're up there."

Carole nodded and did as he suggested, checking the girth while she was at it. Then she took the reins and gave the pony a pat. "Okay, boy," she murmured. "Let's see what you can do."

Remembering how the pony had stepped off with Stan, she kept the reins snug as she swung up into the saddle. Even so, the pony danced to one side. Carole kept her balance, finding the right stirrup quickly.

Whether it was Carole's lighter weight, as Stan had suggested, or just that he had tired himself out, Jinx was slightly calmer than he'd been under the farmhand. He only bucked twice, and he managed to do most of what Carole asked with only moderate protest. Carole took him around the ring for a few minutes, then rode back over to the two men. "He's green," she said breathlessly as she dismounted and handed the reins to Stan so that she could run up the stirrups. "Totally green, with tons of energy. That's all that's wrong with him. I don't think he's trying to be nasty, he just doesn't understand what he's supposed to do."

Max scratched his chin thoughtfully. "I see," he said. Then he turned to the farmhand. "Now, Stan, let me ask you. When Mrs. Rand says she'll only let the two horses go together—"

"She means it," Stan said grimly before Max could finish. "Believe me, Maddie here would be long gone by now if she didn't. We've had four or five buyers willing to pay more than Mrs. R was asking for Maddie alone. Nobody wants to deal with that one, though." He nodded toward Jinx, who had turned his head to bite at the saddle on his back.

Carole bit her lip. *Poor Jinx!* she thought, watching the pony. *Nobody wants you. But it's only because nobody has ever bothered to teach you the right way to behave. I know you could learn if you had the right teacher. . . .* Her mind flashed back to her earlier conversation with Ben. If the two of them worked together, she was sure they could help Jinx live up to his potential.

"Hmmm." Max sighed. "Well, I'm afraid I—"

"Max!" Carole interrupted urgently. "Wait. Can I talk to you for a minute?"

Stan was already lifting the saddle off Jinx's back. "I've got to take this boy in," he said, gesturing toward the barn. "Go ahead and discuss it if you want. I'll be back shortly."

As he headed off with Jinx in tow, Carole looked

pleadingly at Max. "Max, I know you don't think Jinx is right for Pine Hollow," she said. "But I think you should give him a chance. I really think he's a nice pony underneath all that attitude. All he needs is some good, solid, steady training and he could be really great."

Max sighed again. "Carole, Jinx certainly is a nice-looking pony, but he's just not what we need right now. His ground manners are terrible, and he's not much better under saddle. It's obvious he's never been properly trained." He grimaced and shook his head. "I'm not sure we need a horse with that kind of track record at Pine Hollow. Especially now, when we're so crowded already. Why waste a stall on a horse that nobody will be able to ride for weeks, maybe months?"

Carole knew that what Max was saying made sense. He was a businessman, and that meant he had to make decisions based on what was best for Pine Hollow as a whole. Still, she couldn't quite get the pony's alert expression out of her mind. "I hear you," she said. "But we do have a few empty stalls right now. And you were planning to start the expansion immediately, right? Before long there'll be plenty of room. And you wouldn't have to worry about training him—I could do it. I'm sure Ben would help." She was talking very fast, not giving Max a chance to respond. "Besides, it would mean

71

you could have Madison, and she's just about perfect."

Max rubbed his ear. "She is awfully nice," he said, glancing at the mare, who was still standing patiently at the second gate.

"See?" Carole said eagerly. "It would be great. And I swear, I'll take care of Jinx's training myself."

"I don't know." Max looked at her skeptically. "Weren't we just discussing how we don't want you to overdo it? That pony would take up a whole lot of time—time you could spend studying."

Carole winced. Was she ever going to stop paying for that one stupid mistake? "I realize that," she said carefully. "I wouldn't let it interfere with my studying. And like I said, Ben would definitely want to help, and he spends all his time at the stable anyway."

Before Max could respond, Stan reappeared. "Well, folks?" he said, walking toward Madison. "What should I tell Mrs. Rand?"

Max was silent for a long moment, staring at the mare as Stan led her away from the fence. Carole held her breath.

"Tell her I need to think about it," Max said at last. "I'll be in touch in the next couple of days one way or the other."

Stan looked slightly surprised, but he nodded. "Fair enough," he said. "I'll let her know."

Carole let out her breath in a whoosh. *Okay, that wasn't exactly a yes,* she thought, watching Max out of the corner of her eye as they headed for the car. *But it wasn't a no, either. And I'm pretty sure that's a good sign!*

FIVE

5

Callie's heart started to beat a little faster as she walked up a slight rise in the ground and Pine Hollow came into view. Shoving her gloved hands deeper into her coat pockets, she glanced at the parking area. Several vehicles were there, but there was no sign of a certain white sedan with a dent in the left fender.

Whew, Callie thought. *I guess that means he already left.*

She was relieved. She had put off coming to Pine Hollow until as late in the day as possible, hoping to miss George. That had meant Scott couldn't drive her, since he was already primping for his big night out with Lisa. But Callie didn't mind the walk—not if it meant she could work her horse in peace, without constantly looking over her shoulder to see if George was behind her.

There was a spring in her step as she hurried across the yard and into the main building. Suddenly she couldn't wait to get to work with Scooby. *Should I take him out in the woods for a little while?* she wondered. Realizing that it would be getting dark by the time she had him groomed and tacked, she shook her head. *I guess we'll just stick to the indoor ring today,* she decided. *We can do some more of that gymnastics work that got interrupted yesterday.*

As she turned into the stable aisle, Callie glanced at the stall at the end, where Checkers was snuffling the top latch on the stall door. "Stop that, you pest," she chided the horse, pushing his nose back into the stall and refastening the latch. Checkers snorted, then turned away to nose at his water bucket. "And you can drop the innocent act, too," Callie added with a grin.

She was still smiling as she turned around and stepped toward her own horse's stall across the aisle. The half door was closed and latched, but when Callie peered over it, she saw that the stall was empty.

She frowned, wondering if Max had switched stalls. He'd been doing quite a bit of that lately—Pine Hollow had nearly forty usable stalls, but until recently several of them had been used for storage. A population explosion in the town of Willow Creek and the surrounding area meant that more people than ever wanted to ride at Pine Hollow, so Max and his staff had cleared out every stall possible to make room for several new boarders, including Scooby. Even so, there were still several unoccupied stalls, and several more that were temporarily empty while their residents were resting and relaxing on twenty-four-hour turnout.

But a quick glance at the card slipped into a slot on the door assured Callie that this was, indeed, still Scooby's stall. The cards always traveled with the horses so that they were never without identification, except occasionally when Checkers or one of the ponies managed to get one out of its holder and have it as a snack.

"Okay," Callie muttered, hurrying toward the office. "So what's the deal?"

She was halfway across the entryway when Maureen emerged from the locker room, munching on a granola bar. She looked surprised to see Callie. "Oh, hey," she said with a lazy wave. "I thought you weren't coming today. I just turned Scooby out a few minutes ago to let him stretch his legs."

"What?" Callie felt her whole body tense with annoyance. "You turned him out? But I was going to ride him."

Maureen shrugged, not seeming the least bit remorseful about turning out Callie's horse without permission. "He's in the south pasture if you want to go get him." She took another bite of her granola bar and glanced at her watch as she chewed and swallowed. "Better hurry if you want to get anything done before it's time for his dinner."

Callie gritted her teeth, controlling her temper with effort. Yelling at Maureen wouldn't accomplish anything. "Okay," she said tightly. "Um, from now on I'll let you know which days I *won't* be riding, okay?"

"Whatever." Maureen popped the last bite of her granola bar into her mouth and brushed off her hands on her jeans. "Have a nice ride."

Callie headed outside and glanced past the schooling ring to the pastures beyond. The south pasture was the largest one at Pine Hollow. Callie estimated it to be at least twelve or fifteen acres, though just at the moment it seemed twice that size. About half a dozen horses were grazing at the far end, near the woods, and Callie could see Scooby's distinctive spotted coat among them. The space between the gate and the horses looked very big, very open, and somehow dangerous.

Dangerous? Callie thought, disgusted with herself. *That's crazy. All I have to do is walk out there, grab Scooby, and lead him in. Big whoop.*

Somehow, though, she couldn't quite stomach the thought of making that long walk. An image from a nature program she'd seen recently popped into her head: A rabbit had been hopping along through just such a field when an enormous hawk had swooped down and sunk its claws into the rabbit's helpless hide.

Callie shuddered and turned away, hurrying back into the stable building. *Never mind,* she thought, trying to suppress the feeling that she was a total coward and a loser. *Maureen was right. It's too close to dinnertime anyway. I'll just do a few chores and then head out.*

She headed for the tack room, intending to give her saddle a good cleaning. She'd been putting it off for a couple of weeks now, and even though she hadn't been riding much, she didn't want to let it go any longer. Entering the small, crowded, but flawlessly organized tack room, she grabbed saddle soap and a sponge and set them on the top of a wide, flat tack trunk near one of the freestanding saddle horses. As she was pulling her saddle down from its assigned rack, she heard footsteps and someone coming into the room behind her.

Taking a deep breath, she turned, expecting to see Maureen. "George!" she gasped, so startled that the saddle almost slipped out of her grasp. She regained her hold just in time, clutching the large hunk of leather to her chest.

"Hi, Callie!" George said cheerfully. "You're not going riding now, are you? I saw Scooby out in the field."

Callie gulped, her head spinning. What was he

doing here? She'd thought she was safe. "N-No," she blurted out. "Uh, I was just—" She couldn't for the life of her figure out how to finish the sentence.

George glanced behind her, clearly noticing the cleaning equipment for the first time. "Oh!" he said, his small gray eyes lighting up. "Are you cleaning your tack? I'll help you if you want."

George was standing in the doorway, blocking her exit, so Callie glanced frantically over at the second door in the room, which led into the office. "Um, no," she said quickly. "I was just—uh—leaving." Shoving her saddle back onto its rack, she darted for the office door, closing it behind her.

Maureen was sitting at the office desk, her jacket on and her car keys in one hand as she scribbled a note on the calendar with the other. She glanced up at Callie in surprise. "Hi," she said. "I thought you were going riding."

Callie couldn't answer. She still couldn't believe George was here. *It shouldn't be some huge surprise,* she reminded herself, taking a few deep breaths to calm herself. *That car belongs to his mother—he must take the bus or whatever sometimes, right? Anyway, it's probably just a coincidence that he's here so late today. No big deal.*

"Gotta go," she muttered, realizing that Maureen was still staring at her curiously.

"Whatever," she heard Maureen say behind her.

Callie darted out of the office and down the hall to the women's bathroom, not daring to look back to see if George was emerging from the tack room. She stayed in there for a good ten minutes, trying to calm down and convince herself that this was not a big deal.

I can't let George Wheeler run my life, she told herself firmly, staring into her own blue eyes in the mirror. *No matter what mistakes I may have made in the beginning, this is getting ridiculous. I already asked him to stay away from me. And then I told him to stay away from me. He's not staying away. So I guess I just have to deal with that somehow.*

She wasn't sure how, short of begging her parents to move to another state, or at least changing schools and moving Scooby to another stable. But she really didn't want to do that. She liked Fenton Hall, the private school she and Scott attended. And she loved Pine Hollow.

So I'll just have to adjust, I guess, she thought, feeling rather helpless. She didn't like the feeling—she preferred being in control of her own life—but she didn't see that she had much choice. It was a free country, and she certainly couldn't stop George from talking to her, could she? It wasn't just that the guy couldn't take a hint, he was oblivious to a virtual two-by-four upside the head.

Callie was starting to feel a little foolish about

standing around in a cold, dimly lit bathroom worrying about whether or not someone would decide to speak to her again. *Enough is enough,* she thought, squaring her shoulders and heading for the door. She would just clean out her cubby and then call it a day.

The student locker room was empty when she entered. She smiled with relief, then walked over and sat down in front of her square wooden cubby on the long bench that ran the length of the room. Her cubby was already fairly neat—Callie liked to keep things organized—but there were a few things she wanted to take home and wash. She dug out her navy schooling breeches and a T-shirt that a horse had slobbered on, then remembered that she'd also left a pair of muddy socks in there a couple of weeks earlier.

"Where are they?" she muttered, leaning farther forward as she dug beneath a neat stack of clothing.

"Did you lose something, Callie?"

Callie jumped, almost banging her head on the top of the cubby. She spun around and saw George standing in the middle of the room. He had changed out of his riding boots into a pair of sneakers, and she hadn't even heard him come in.

"What do you want?" She realized her voice sounded nasty, but she didn't care.

George looked surprised. "I just came in to get

my coat," he said, hurrying toward his own cubby. "So what are you up to tonight? Heading home soon?"

Callie hesitated. She was strangely reluctant to answer, and not just because it was none of George's business. Her parents were out at another political event that evening, and Scott would be out on his date until late. Callie wasn't relishing the thought of walking home through the cold, dark winter night. Or of entering her empty house and being there alone for hours. "I—I—" she stammered, wondering why she suddenly felt so nervous, almost fearful. She should just tell George to go away and leave her alone. Again. But she couldn't quite manage it.

"Are you okay?" George took a step closer, peering at her intently. "Callie?"

"I'm fine," Callie replied, struggling to sound normal even as she took a step back, banging her calf into the bench behind her. "Fine. I—"

"Hey, I thought I heard voices in here."

"Stevie!" Callie had never been so glad to see anyone in her life. "Hi! I didn't know you were still here."

"Ditto." Stevie glanced curiously at George. "Hey," she said. "I thought you took off a while ago."

George shrugged and smiled. "I came back. Um,

but I'd better get going now. See you." He hurried out of the room, pulling on his coat as he went.

Stevie blinked and stared after him. "What's with him?" she asked as she leaned over and dragged her winter jacket out of her own messy cubby. "I hope he's not getting sick of all my questions about eventing already." She winked at Callie. "Because I've got about a million more of 'em."

Callie returned her smile weakly. "I don't know." She felt a little better now that George had gone. But soon Stevie would go, too. And then what? Callie couldn't hang around Pine Hollow all night, especially since George was liable to pop up again just when she thought she was safe. And as much as she hated to admit it, even to herself, she was feeling a little spooked about returning to her empty house—especially whenever she thought about glimpsing that pale, round face pressed up against the window. "Um, so what are you up to tonight?" she asked Stevie, stalling for time.

"My parents are going to dinner and a play tonight, and it's Alex's turn to cook, which means TV-dinner time." Stevie wrinkled her nose. Then her eyes lit up and she grinned. "So how about it? Want to grab a burger or something?"

"Absolutely," Callie said immediately. "In fact, that's the best idea I've heard all day."

"I can't believe you've never been here before," Stevie commented, dipping a french fry into the blob of ketchup on her plate. "Everybody knows the Creekside Grill has the best burgers in town."

Stevie was in a good mood. It had been an interesting day at the stable, and she was at one of her favorite restaurants. Just about the only thing keeping her from being totally happy was the knowledge that there were only two more days before school started again. It seemed unfair, especially when she was just getting into the swing of her new eventing training.

Callie swallowed a bite of her burger. "The food *is* good," she said, glancing around the casual wood-paneled restaurant and wiping her chin. "I guess this just isn't the kind of place where Dad usually entertains his big-money campaign contributors or holds press conferences," she said teasingly.

Stevie grinned. "Anyway," she said, "like I was saying, I was kind of worried about whether Belle would be up for something like this. She's not really bred for jumping, you know? But George says—" Was it her imagination, or did Callie wince slightly at the mention of George's name? Stevie had noticed it once or twice already since they'd left the stable half an hour earlier. She cleared her throat and continued. "George says it won't matter much at the beginning levels. It's not like we'll be facing any huge fences to start with."

"That makes sense." Callie stared at the plate in front of her, her expression neutral.

Stevie forgot about Callie's reaction as she thought about her plans. "Anyway, we should be okay with the dressage part—I haven't been schooling as much as I should lately, but the tests will be a lot easier than the ones we're used to from dressage shows and stuff anyhow. So it's mostly the jumping we've got to focus on, especially the cross-country jumping. I haven't really done much of that for a long time, and Belle hasn't done much more than hop a few logs on the trail. But George promised to give us some pointers."

"That's good."

This time Stevie couldn't help noticing that Callie *had* cringed slightly at George's name. She frowned. Callie had been having a difficult time with George because of his hopeless crush and everything—Stevie knew that well enough—but she hadn't realized it was quite this bad. Was Callie so sensitive about what had happened that she couldn't even stand the sound of George's name? Was Stevie going to have to be careful never to mention her new eventing consultant in Callie's presence? She didn't like the thought of having to censor herself like that.

Not exactly the most relaxing way to have a conversation, she thought ruefully. *Still, Callie's my friend—if she needs a little longer to get over this, I've got to remember to make the effort.* She just hoped she could manage it. When she was excited about something, like she was now about eventing, she tended to sort of forget about everything else.

"Anyway," she said, swishing another french fry through the ketchup, "the first thing I need to do is make sure Belle's in good shape so we can start some refresher jumping training."

As Callie started to answer, saying something about conditioning, Stevie happened to glance in the direction of the door. To her surprise, she saw a familiar pudgy figure entering. "Hey!" she blurted out. "Yo, George!" She waved, then winced. *Oops.*

George spotted them immediately, his apple-cheeked face stretching into a big smile. Returning Stevie's wave, he hurried toward their table.

Callie stared fixedly at the table in front of her. Her face looked strangely pale.

"Sorry," Stevie said quietly, smiling apologetically and feeling guilty. "Guess I should've kept quiet, huh?"

George reached them before Callie could respond. "Hi, you two!" he said, beaming at them cheerfully. "Fancy meeting you here. It's a small world."

"It's a small town," Stevie corrected him.

George glanced at her half-eaten burger. "Wow, that looks good," he said. "I'm starved. Mind if I join you?"

"Um . . ." Stevie shot another quick look at Callie. Part of her was tempted to just agree. She really did have a ton of questions for George, and this would be the perfect opportunity to pick his brain.

But the thought barely crossed her mind before she knew she couldn't do it. *It's not like I'm never allowed to speak to George again just because I'm friends with Callie,* she told herself. *But that doesn't mean I should invite him to sit down and eat with us.*

"Sorry," she told George, who was already pulling out a chair. "This is sort of a private dinner tonight. You know—girl stuff. Maybe another time, okay?"

"Oh!" George looked startled. His cheeks turned pink, and he glanced quickly from Stevie to Callie and back again. "Um, that's okay. I understand."

He scurried away, disappearing through the door a moment later. Stevie watched him go, feeling bad about hurting his feelings. *Oh well,* she thought. *What choice did I have?*

She turned back to face Callie, who was still staring at the table. "So I guess this means things still aren't going well with you two," Stevie said bluntly. "What's the latest?"

Callie shrugged. "There is no latest," she said

quickly, barely meeting Stevie's gaze before her eyes skittered away toward the door. "No big deal. I just didn't feel like putting up with him tonight, that's all."

"Really?" Stevie couldn't help feeling a little skeptical. She and Callie hadn't been friends for all that long, but she thought she knew her pretty well. And she had the funniest feeling that there was more to the story than Callie was telling her.

This time Callie met her gaze full on. "Really," she said firmly. "Let's just drop it, okay?"

Stevie shrugged. "Okay." But she wasn't sure she meant that. Something didn't seem okay about the whole situation at all.

SIX

"How's your pasta?" Scott asked, leaning forward and smiling at Lisa.

Lisa finished chewing the bite in her mouth. "Really good," she said. "It's—"

"Yo! Forester!" someone called from across the crowded diner.

Scott glanced over toward the voice and grinned. "Hey, Ward," he called back, raising a hand in greeting. "How's it going?"

With some effort Lisa refrained from rolling her eyes. As much as she loved the food at the Magnolia Diner, she was really starting to wish she hadn't suggested it that evening. It was Friday night, and as usual the place was hopping. There weren't many places to go on a casual date in Willow Creek—most of the restaurants were either fuddy-duddy white-napkin kinds of places or greasy fast-food joints. Along with a couple of pizza places and the Creekside Grill, the popular Magnolia Diner was a magnet for people Lisa's age, especially on weekends. The problem was, just about everyone who came in seemed to find it necessary to stop by their table to say hello to Scott.

Even that wouldn't be so bad, she thought, poking at her fettucine with her fork, *if Scott didn't feel the need to have a nice, long, personal chat with every single one of them.*

Noticing that Scott had turned back to her with his usual easy smile, she pasted a pleasant expression on her face. She was trying not to let Scott's sociable nature bother her—after all, it wasn't as though it was any huge surprise—but for some reason, it was wearing on her nerves that night.

It also wouldn't be so bad if Scott seemed to mind all the interruptions to our date, even a little bit, she thought. *If he really wanted to be with me, wouldn't he be a little more focused on, well, me?*

"By the way, Lisa," Scott said, leaning forward again. "In case I didn't mention it before, I'm really glad to be here with you tonight."

At that, Lisa relaxed slightly, wondering if she was being too uptight. After all, Scott hadn't really done anything so terrible. He was just being polite to all those other people. *She* was the one he'd asked out. Her heart fluttered as she gazed into his sincere blue eyes. "Me too," she said softly.

"Good." Scott smiled. "Because I hope we—"

"Forester! Hey, man, what's up?"

Lisa grimaced as what had seemed to be turning into a special moment dissipated, lost once again in the action and clamor of the diner around them. She looked up and saw that a Fenton Hall junior named Kenny Lamb was loping toward their table, a grin on his angular face.

Scott raised a hand in greeting. "Hey, Kenny."

Kenny skidded to a stop at their table, tossing his long brown bangs out of his eyes. "Hey," he replied, barely bothering to glance Lisa's way before returning his attention to Scott. "So dude, did you hear what Jimbo did to his folks' cabin on New Year's Eve?"

With that, the two of them launched off into the latest gossip about one of their classmates. Since Lisa didn't even go to Fenton Hall—she, along with Carole, attended Willow Creek's public high school—her mind drifted quickly. Once again, she found herself pondering Scott's sociable nature.

Is this sort of situation something I really want to deal with on a regular basis? she wondered. *I mean, if I'm getting annoyed already, what does that mean for the future? Is this the kind of thing I'd get used to after a while, or will it just get worse? Or am I being stupid to even think about this becoming anything serious?*

Lisa sat back and thought about that. Both she

and Scott would be starting college the next fall—just eight months away now. Lisa already knew where she was going. She'd been accepted early into Northern Virginia University, a good local school about forty miles from Willow Creek. Scott wasn't quite as good a student as she was, but she knew he'd applied to a long list of top schools, most of which were hundreds of miles away. What if they ended up as a real couple, and he ended up somewhere like Yale or Northwestern, too far away even to visit most weekends?

Okay, this is just a tad premature, Lisa reminded herself, realizing she'd let her mind drift way off course as she waited for Scott to finish his conversation. Sipping her water, she did her best to smile pleasantly as Kenny pounded on the table, apparently to express his amusement at whatever Scott had just said. *I mean, judging by tonight, it doesn't seem like Scott cares much about being with me at all.*

She realized that was a little unfair. Scott was a social person—that was just the way he was made. He had a gift for connecting with people, all sorts of people, all the time. It was the same gift that had won his father a seat in Congress, and Lisa knew that it was a big part of what made Scott, Scott. She just couldn't help wishing he wouldn't be quite so . . . well, Scott-like when he was supposed to be out with her.

"Okay, dude," Kenny said at last, slapping Scott on the shoulder. "I'd better get back to my buddies, or they'll scarf all my buffalo wings."

"See you." Scott waved as the other guy departed, then turned to Lisa with a smile. "Hey," he said, noticing that Lisa had barely touched her food. "What's the matter? I thought you liked your dinner."

"What? Oh, sure." Lisa forced a smile. "Just taking a break. You know, digesting."

He doesn't mean anything bad by it, she thought as she busied herself with her food, not wanting Scott to guess what she was thinking. *He's just being himself. It doesn't mean he isn't that interested in our date—or me. It's just different, that's all.*

That was what she really needed to digest. That Scott wasn't, and never would be, Alex. They were both great guys—cute, smart, interesting, and fun. But in many ways they were polar opposites. Sometimes when she was out with Alex, it had been as if the rest of the world had ceased to exist for both of them. Scott made her feel special, but not in the same way. Not in that intense, singular, totally focused way that Alex always had.

I know I shouldn't compare them, she thought, sneaking a glance at Scott out of the corner of her eye. *I know I should accept Scott for who he is and not expect him to treat me exactly like Alex did.* At that moment someone else yelled Scott's name, and Lisa sighed, steeling herself for another long pause in their date. *That's just kind of hard to remember sometimes.*

Carole found herself humming softly under her breath as she walked from stall to stall, checking to be sure that all the horses had finished their evening meals and were doing all right. Things were winding down for the night at Pine Hollow—all the riders and boarders had gone home, and Max was up at the house, tucking his daughters into bed. Carole had always loved this time of the evening at the stable. It always felt so safe and cozy to her, like all was right with the world.

Finally she reached Checkers' stall at the end of the aisle. "How're you doing, boy?" Carole asked as the friendly gelding came forward to sniff at her curiously, clearly hoping for treats. She scratched him on the jaw instead, then checked to make sure he hadn't been messing with the latches on his door. Giving him one last pat, she glanced at her watch.

Dad won't be home for another couple of hours, she thought, remembering that her father had mentioned a benefit dinner he had to attend that evening. Since retiring from the Marine Corps several years earlier, Colonel Hanson had become active on the boards of several charitable organizations, which often required his appearance at some social function or another. *I might as well stick around here and get some work done,* Carole thought. *Someone needs to refill the grain bin, and the lesson saddles are a mess. . . .*

Still ticking off tasks in her head, she wandered across the entryway toward the tack room, enjoying the unusual feeling of having the stable more or less to herself. Maureen had the evening off—she had left ages ago. Red and Denise were still on their honeymoon. Max had gone up to the house for dinner and family time earlier, though he would be back at some point for a final check. Ben was probably still around somewhere—he rarely left the stable before nine o'clock at night—but Carole hadn't seen him in half an hour.

Maybe he took off, too. After all, it is Friday night, she thought, a shadow of self-pity creeping over her good mood. *Most people have things to do. Not to mention people to do them with.*

She shook her head fiercely, not wanting to think about Cam. Not now, when she was feeling so happy about being back at work. Because that happiness was the only thing keeping her from brooding over what had happened—how the guy she'd thought was in love with her had turned around and betrayed her—and she didn't want to do that. Not now.

Deciding that a calming physical task like cleaning tack would help to take her mind off that, she hurried into the tack room. After straightening up—as usual, that day's lesson kids had returned half the bridles to the wrong hooks and left saddle pads draped everywhere—she set out her cleaning supplies and then walked over to pull down the closest saddle. As she turned around, she saw Ben standing in the doorway watching her.

"Oh!" Carole said, startled. For some reason, she found herself blushing. "Um, hi there. I wasn't sure if you were still here or not."

"I'm here." As usual, Ben's dark eyes were unreadable. Carole half expected him to turn around and leave as quickly as he could. "Um, want some help?"

For a second, Carole wasn't sure what he meant. Then, remembering the saddle she was still clutching, she smiled tentatively. "You mean you want to—uh, that is, sure. Thanks."

Ben nodded. Without another word, he turned to grab another saddle. Soon the two of them were working side by side at a pair of saddle horses, rubbing saddle soap into the well-worn leather. Usually Ben's quiet nature made Carole want to talk more just to fill the void. But that night, his wordlessness seemed easier to accept somehow. In fact, it felt almost friendly. The two of them worked in companionable silence for a few minutes, the only sound the squeaking of leather as they worked on the saddles.

Finally Ben glanced up and cleared his throat. "Carole . . ."

"Yes?" she said quickly, wondering what he was thinking that suddenly made him look so serious.

Ben coughed. "Oh. Uh, did you give Patch his bute yet?"

"Uh-huh. And his foot's looking a lot better today."

"Good." The ghost of a smile flitted across Ben's face. "The beginners have been bugging Max about him. Even heard one of them saying she was going to send him a get-well card."

Carole grinned. "Let me guess. That would be Mandy Fredericks?"

"Yep." Ben smiled back briefly before returning his attention to his work.

Carole was a little surprised by how comfortable it felt to be there alone with Ben. He had a tendency to make most people feel uncomfortable in his presence—his dark, critical gaze and forbidding silence were enough to chase most people away within moments. Besides that, Carole was feeling pretty raw and vulnerable after what had happened with Cam. It had only been three days, and she knew it would take a lot longer than that for her to regain her trust in people. But talking with her friends on their trail ride the day before had helped a lot. And hanging out with Ben was helping, too. He was being so nice and non-Ben-like that he almost seemed like another friend helping her in her time of need.

But that's silly, she reminded herself, leaning over a spot on the saddle's skirt. *Ben probably never even noticed I was going out with Cam in the first place. Let alone realized we've broken up now. Whatever's behind his personality change, I'm sure it has nothing to do with me, unless he's just glad I'm finally back doing my share of the work around here.*

After a while, as Carole returned one clean saddle to its rack and grabbed another, her thoughts turned away from Ben's intriguing new attitude and back toward her latest preoccupation. "Hey," she said to Ben as she set the new saddle on her saddle horse, "did you hear about those two horses Max and I looked at this afternoon?"

Ben glanced at her. "Yeah."

He didn't elaborate. Carole wasn't sure whether that was a good sign or a bad one. She took a deep breath. "Do you know if Max is really considering them?" she asked. Ben might not talk to people much, but he was always around. He might have heard something she hadn't.

"Don't know," Ben said with a shrug. "He didn't say."

"Oh." Carole sighed, remembering the look in

Jinx's eyes—and also remembering the way he'd bucked and kicked and generally carried on. "I mean, Max told me he would think about it, but I don't know. I'm afraid he was just humoring me because he knows I liked them. One of them is this pony with some issues." With that, she launched into a detailed description of Jinx and her test ride.

Ben listened quietly, still scrubbing his saddle. "Sounds like he needs a good sacking out, to start," he said when Carole had finished.

She nodded. "Definitely," she agreed. "That, and then a review of all the basics, starting with yielding to pressure on the ground and working his way back up to the under-saddle stuff. I mean, basically I would want to start all over again as if he were a foal just learning the basics for the first time. We could start out working in the halter, dealing with handling and grooming and leading and that stuff, and then move on to longeing. . . ." This time she went on to describe everything she'd been thinking about Jinx's problems and how to solve them.

Once again, Ben waited until she'd finished. "Did you tell Max that?"

"What?" Carole blinked, slightly confused. She was still thinking about all the potential the pony had. Potential that had been totally wasted so far but was still there, waiting for someone like Carole to set it free.

Ben was watching her. "Your plans. Step by step. Did you tell Max?"

"Oh. Sure." Carole paused, thinking about that. "Well, no," she amended. "Not exactly. I mean, I told him I thought I could really help turn him into something nice, but I guess I didn't go into that much detail." She shrugged. "Max knows the process, though."

Ben nodded slowly, not saying anything. Carole frowned slightly, wondering what he was thinking. *Doesn't he think Max knows how to train a horse?* she thought. *Get real. He's probably done it dozens, if not hundreds, of times. Max could probably retrain Jinx in his sleep, if he weren't so busy with the expansion plans and all the new students and everything.*

Glancing at Ben, she saw that he had returned his attention to the saddle he was cleaning. His hands moved the sponge expertly, automatically. Soon he was finished, and he hoisted the saddle and traded it for another. Carole blinked, suddenly realizing something.

Back when I first started riding, I had no idea how to go about cleaning a saddle, she remembered. *And even when I learned, it took me ages to do it—not to mention that I made a few mistakes along the way, like the time I saddle soaped the suede knee rolls on one of the pony saddles.* She blushed slightly as she remembered that incident, which had taken place when she was about six years old. *But now I can do it in a matter of minutes with one hand tied behind my back.*

She looked over at Ben again. He was focused on his work, but he glanced up and caught her gaze. "Training that pony will be a lot of work," he said suddenly. "If you need help . . ."

"Thanks." Carole smiled gratefully. "I'm sure I will. If I can convince Max to give me—us—a shot at it."

To Max, retraining Jinx would be as natural as cleaning a saddle is to Ben or me, she thought. *But he doesn't have time to do it himself, and he's worried that we don't know how to go about it.*

"So all I have to do," she continued the thought aloud, "is let him know that we know what to do. That we have a plan." She realized she hadn't been doing that so far. Instead, she had spent most of the ride home from Mrs. Rand's farm giving Max some variation of "Pleeeeeez, let me try!"

That kind of pleading and whining is never going to impress Max, she thought, picking up the saddle she'd just finished. *But presenting him with a plan of action might do the trick. Especially if I also remind him that I do have at least a little bit of a track record training horses—I brought Starlight along from a green four-year-old to the horse he is now, and Ben and I have made a lot of progress with Firefly this year, too.*

She glanced at Ben, wondering if he realized how

much he'd just helped her. Even though he hadn't really said much, somehow he'd given her a whole new perspective on the Jinx issue. She opened her mouth, trying to find the words to thank him.

She forgot about that when she heard the sound of footsteps on the wooden floorboards of the office next door. "That must be Max," she said, suddenly eager to put her new plan into action. She dropped the clean saddle on its rack and headed for the door. "Wish me luck!"

SEVEN
7

Stevie hit her turn signal as she approached the exit of the shopping center's parking lot. She hummed along with the radio as she waited for a break in traffic, squinting slightly against the brightness of the other cars' headlights. It was already fully dark out—she and Callie had spent more time at that restaurant than she'd realized.

She sure got chatty all of a sudden after that thing with George, she thought as she pulled out onto the road. *It was like she wanted to hang out all night.* Stevie smothered a yawn, glancing at the clock on her dashboard, which read 10:42 A.M. She grimaced, making a mental note to reset it when she got home.

Though she still felt bad about the way George had taken off, Stevie was glad that Callie seemed to be feeling better. Besides, she could talk to George any time. She planned to track him down the next day to follow up on a few things they'd discussed earlier.

It was really nice of him to offer to take me over to the cross-country course at the show grounds next week, she thought, recalling a conversation they'd had while cleaning tack that afternoon. Pine Hollow had a few fences out in the fields and on the trails, but it didn't have anything like a real cross-country course. *I hope they have one of those bank step thingies there,* Stevie thought, making a mental note to ask George the proper name for that type of jump. *I really want to figure out—*

"Yikes!" she exclaimed aloud, snapping out of her thoughts as someone darted into the road just a few yards in front of her.

Spinning the wheel to one side, she jammed her foot on the brake. The car skidded to a stop just six feet or so from the pedestrian, who seemed oblivious to all danger.

"Idiot," Stevie muttered, her heart beating fast and furious as she clutched the steering wheel with relief. That had been close.

Wondering who would be stupid enough to step out in front of a fast-moving car, she peered at the pedestrian, who had turned around and was holding up one hand against the brightness of Stevie's headlights. She could see that it was a young woman, slender and dressed in a very short skirt despite the cold night. The woman had long red hair and was holding a cigarette. As Stevie squinted at her, she realized that she looked an awful lot like—

"Maureen?" Stevie murmured uncertainly.

At that moment the woman lowered her hand, weaving tipsily from side to side as she headed back toward the sidewalk. Stevie could see plainly that it was, indeed, Pine Hollow's newest stable hand. And from the way she was acting, she wasn't even aware that she'd just missed getting run down. In fact, she didn't seem to be aware of too much at the moment.

"Yikes," Stevie whispered. Maureen was staggering toward a local dive called Houdini's. Stevie didn't know much about the bar except that it tended to attract kind of a rough crowd. "So this is where she hangs out on her nights off?"

As she reached the sidewalk, Maureen paused and took a drag off her cigarette. Seeming to notice Stevie's car for the first time, she grinned and waved the cigarette at it in a sort of boozy salute. Stevie had no idea if the stable hand had recognized her or not—it was dark, and Maureen didn't seem to be in a terribly observant mood—but either way, she didn't bother to wave back. Instead she continued slowly on her way.

So that's the person who's helping take care of my horse? Stevie thought in disgust as she reached the corner. She glanced in her rearview mirror and saw that several men had emerged from the bar and joined Maureen. All of them seemed to be dancing on the sidewalk in front of the bar. Stevie could hear their laughing and hollering even half a block away with her windows rolled up.

Still, however Maureen chose to let off steam on her own time, Stevie reminded herself that she'd never behaved that way at Pine Hollow. Aside from sneaking a cigarette once in the women's bathroom, the new stable hand had seemed to be a conscientious, hardworking employee. Of course, there was the constant flirting, too, but that wasn't really a big deal. At least not as far as the horses were concerned.

Anyway, that's kind of how people are, Stevie thought. Though she was well past the bar by now, she kept her speed down, still spooked by the close call. *They aren't usually all good or all bad—more like a combination of both. Sort of like George. Callie acts like he's the devil, and from her perspective he really is pretty obnoxious, following her around and mooning over her all the time, even though she's made it perfectly clear that she's not interested. Because of all that, she just can't see the sweet, helpful side of him that I saw tonight. It's a shame, really. They could both be missing out on a really nice friendship.*

She thought about the other people she knew. There had been a few times when she'd been sure she wasn't going to like someone but changed her mind after getting to know them better. For instance, Max's wife, Deborah, had seemed uptight and unlikable when she'd first arrived at Pine Hollow years earlier. But it had turned out she'd just been nervous and in love. As soon as she relaxed, her true personality had emerged and Stevie had been crazy about her ever since. Then there had been Stevie's ninth-grade English teacher, who had started off seeming like a real dragon lady but ended up being one of Stevie's all-time favorite teachers at Fenton Hall.

Of course, sometimes it works the other way around, too, she reminded herself, thinking of Carole's recent experience with Cam. *Sometimes a person seems great at first but turns out to be totally vile.*

Suddenly noticing lights glaring in her rearview, Stevie glanced at the speedometer and realized she'd slowed to near a crawl. Feeling slightly foolish, she pressed down on the accelerator until she'd reached a more normal speed.

Anyway, she reminded herself, still thinking about Cam's despicable behavior on New Year's Eve, *I suppose anyone can have a bad night once in a while, like Carole did the other night. I don't know anything about Maureen's personal life—for all I know, her boyfriend might have just dumped her and she's drowning her sorrows. Not the smartest decision in the world, maybe, especially if she keeps trying to get herself run over. But understandable.*

At that, her mind drifted back to her own younger days. Over the years, Stevie herself had made a lot of decisions and done a lot of things that might have seemed stupid to other people. Her parents, her teachers, Max, and many others had sometimes failed to appreciate her exuberance and impulsiveness, which had all too frequently landed Stevie—and sometimes her friends as well—in hot water.

So maybe Maureen and I have something in common, she thought, staring ahead at the road as it sped by beneath the beam of her headlights. *Maybe she's just being herself, for better or for worse.*

She grimaced as she remembered how Maureen had swayed drunkenly back toward the bar. In this particular case, there seemed to be a lot less better than worse. But whatever was going on with Maureen, Stevie decided to keep an open mind about it, at least until she got to know her better.

Callie was peering under her bed, searching for her mysteriously missing chemistry notebook, when the phone rang. For all her stalling back at that restaurant with Stevie, she hadn't managed to avoid coming home to an empty house—her parents were still out, and so was Scott. For a moment she was tempted to let the answering machine pick up. But then, feeling annoyed at her own jumpiness, she hurried to get it. She just hoped it wasn't Stevie. She already felt bad about lying to her earlier—she had seemed so concerned. But Callie just hadn't been able to bring herself to admit the truth.

"Hello?" she said, still a little distracted by the missing notebook. Where could it be? She was almost positive she'd brought it home before the holidays.

There was a slight pause on the other end. "Hello?" an unfamiliar, slightly high pitched voice responded at last. "Er, is this Callie Forester?"

"Who's calling?" Callie said automatically.

"I'm looking for Callie Forester," the voice insisted scratchily. "Is this Callie?"

Callie's grip on the phone tightened. Suddenly forgetting all about her notebook, she frowned suspiciously. "Who is this?" she demanded.

"I'm looking for Callie Forester," the voice replied. "Is this Callie Forester?"

Without another word, Callie slammed the phone down, her hands shaking. *George,* she thought numbly. *It had to be George, disguising his voice. But why? What does he want with me?*

That was the question of the hour. What in the world was he after? She'd made it clear on more than one occasion that she wanted nothing more to do with him. So why couldn't he just take the hint and leave her alone?

She leaned against the wall, staring at the now silent phone and willing herself to relax. There was no point in jumping to conclusions—she didn't even know for a fact that it was really George. For all she knew it could have been some salesperson calling to try to convince her to apply for a credit card or change her long-distance carrier, but it was a little late for a call like that. Still, there was no reason the call couldn't have been perfectly legitimate.

But the more she tried to convince herself of that, the more certain she felt that it had, indeed, been George calling. Maybe he'd just wanted to see if she was there. Maybe he'd been calling from somewhere nearby and was even now sneaking up to peer in through her window. . . .

"Don't be stupid," she whispered aloud. But she couldn't seem to stop herself from creeping over to her bedroom window. Pulling back the curtain slightly, she peered out into the dark, moonless night. Was George out there somewhere? Was he looking back at her right that very minute?

The thought made her jump. She was tempted to race downstairs to the basement and lock herself in. At least there weren't any windows down there.

But at that moment she caught a glimpse of headlights turning onto her street. As the car came closer, she recognized it as her father's dark blue sedan.

She relaxed immediately, relief washing over her so strongly that her knees felt weak. Hurrying downstairs, she was waiting in the front hall when her parents walked in, flushed from the cold and chatting about the dinner they'd just attended.

"Callie!" her father said when he spotted her. He shrugged off his wool coat and turned to hang it in the closet. "What are you up to?"

"Nothing much," Callie said, trying to sound normal. She didn't want her parents to know how freaked out she'd been—she'd been trying all along not to make a bigger deal of the whole George situation than it deserved. That included not telling her parents a thing about it, though it was getting harder and harder to keep her feelings hidden. "I was just getting my stuff together for school on Monday."

Mrs. Forester shook her head in amazement. "Is school starting again already?" she said, unwinding her cashmere scarf and tucking it into her coat pocket. "It seems like your school vacations get shorter every year."

"Maybe the four of us can go out Sunday night to kick off the semester," Callie's father suggested. "I could probably cut my meetings in New York this weekend a little short and get back in time for a late dinner."

"You're going to New York this weekend?" Callie

suddenly realized that this could be her salvation. "Can I come?"

Her mother blinked at her in surprise. "You want to go to New York with your father?" she said. "But I thought you'd want to spend every last precious moment of vacation at the stable, as usual."

Callie smiled weakly. "Um, I'll have plenty of time for training and stuff after school starts. I just thought maybe I could do some shopping while Dad's working—you know, kick back for a couple of days before the daily grind starts up again."

"Hey, I'm not going to argue," her father said, putting an arm around her shoulders and hugging her. "I'd love to spend a weekend in New York with my favorite daughter. Just promise me you won't drag me into every shoe store in Manhattan."

"Deal." Callie followed her parents down the hall toward the kitchen, feeling relieved. She knew she was copping out, but she just couldn't deal with her life in Willow Creek anymore at the moment. A couple of days away might be just what she needed to get a handle on things.

EIGHT

That Monday morning, Stevie spotted Callie hurrying across Fenton Hall's spacious, stuffy-portrait-lined lobby. "Yo! Callie!" she called, waving. She raced to catch up as her friend paused and looked back at her.

"Hi, Stevie," Callie said as Stevie skidded to a stop in front of her.

"Hey." Stevie noticed that Callie's face looked a bit strained. "How was the Big Apple?" She'd heard from Scott about Callie's weekend trip to New York City.

"It was okay. Did some shopping, saw a play. The usual." Callie's words were normal enough, but her expression still seemed a little odd.

She's probably just bummed to be back at school, just like me, Stevie thought. Another possibility flitted briefly across her mind—*This couldn't have anything to do with George, could it?*—but she shrugged it off. Just because Callie hadn't wanted to hang out

113

with him the other night, it didn't mean she was obsessed with him at all times.

"Anyway," Stevie said, "you missed an interesting weekend at the stable. Somehow Carole convinced Max to buy these two horses they went and looked at—did she tell you about them?"

Callie shook her head, glancing over her shoulder distractedly. "I don't think so."

"One of them sounds like a nice school horse, but the other one is some terror of a Welsh pony with a bad attitude and next to no training. Naturally, that second one is the one Carole fell in love with." Stevie smiled and rolled her eyes. "She talked Max into letting her work with this pony, and he— Hey, are you okay?" She blinked at Callie, noticing that she was glancing around the lobby and looking oddly nervous. "What are you looking for?"

"Huh?" Callie looked at her. "Oh. Um, sorry. I was listening. New pony."

"Right." Stevie couldn't help noticing that Callie hadn't really answered her question. Once again George's face floated briefly into her mind. "Um, anyway, I guess the old owner is bringing the horses over this afternoon. Max is going to have them vetted at Pine Hollow, and if they pass, we'll have them on a trial basis until he figures out whether the pony will ever—"

"Stevie! Stevie Lake! Over here!"

Glancing up, Stevie saw the editor of the school newspaper waving to her from the other end of the crowded lobby. "Hey, there's Theresa," she said, suddenly distracted with the thought of all the article ideas she'd come up with over vacation. Getting back to work on her budding journalism career was just about the only good part of coming back to school. She gave Callie a quick pat on the arm. "I'll talk to you at lunch, okay?"

Callie was having more and more trouble controlling her nervousness as she made her way through the narrow, crowded second-floor hallway to her homeroom. She'd thought that Stevie would never stop talking—standing there, exposed and vulnerable, in the middle of the lobby like that had been a horrible feeling, though she hadn't wanted to admit as much to Stevie. Even now that she was free, with just half the length of the hallway standing between herself and her homeroom, she still felt jumpy and uneasy.

Now I know what a fox hunt must feel like from the fox's perspective, she thought wryly, ducking around a knot of freshman girls giggling near the water fountain.

She paused in front of the girls' bathroom, wondering if she had time before the bell to stop in and splash cold water on her face. Meanwhile her eyes continued to dart around at the other people in the hall, searching for a certain familiar face. Suddenly she caught a glimpse of a wisp of pale blond hair poking up over the heads of some other girls nearby.

George! she thought frantically. *It's George! I know it!*

Her panic took over, and she spun around like a spooked horse and bolted into the bathroom, nearly bowling over a pair of sophomores who were emerging. They shot her dirty looks, but Callie hardly noticed. She collapsed against the counter, feeling borderline hysterical. She had no idea if that had actually been George out there. He wasn't the only person at Fenton Hall with that shade of hair, and she hadn't stuck around long enough to see anything else.

This is ridiculous, she thought. *Even if it was him, so what? There were like a million other people out there. What's he going to do to me? What has he ever done to me, really, when you get right down to it, except be a pest and talk to me when I don't want him to?*

The image of that pale round face squashed against the window swam into her mind, but she banished it. What proof did she have that that had really been George, either? Maybe the whole incident had been a product of her overactive imagination. Maybe all she'd seen out there in the dark was a large moth beating its wings against the lighted window.

Callie turned and cranked the handle on the sink, which was just as ancient and creaky as everything else at Fenton Hall. Cold water spurted out, and Callie bent over and splashed it on her face and neck. Standing and glancing into the mirror above the sink, she grabbed a paper towel and dabbed off the moisture.

"There, that's better," she muttered, pushing back a few stray tendrils of her hair. "Much better."

She glanced at the door, willing herself to walk over and go through it. But at the thought of the crowded hallway outside, she cringed back against the sink, shuddering. How could she possibly make her way through the hordes of people? George might be right up on her before she could spot him.

She was the only one left in the bathroom, which meant that it was almost time for the bell. Maybe she should just wait until the bell rang—the hallways would clear out quickly, and she could make her escape then. Of course, if she was more than a few seconds late, her homeroom teacher would probably give her a detention. Still, that didn't seem like such a bad thing when she considered the alternative. In fact, detention sounded downright safe and cozy right about then.

The bell rang shrilly, making her jump. *Okay,*

now I'm officially late anyway, she thought, strangely relieved to have the decision taken out of her hands. *Might as well hang out for a couple of minutes and regain my composure.*

She walked over to the window and glanced out at the winter sky, which was covered in gloomy-looking steel gray clouds. Leaning against the wall, she concentrated on taking deep, even breaths until she was sure her heartbeat was back to normal. Then she returned to the sinks, checking her hair and repairing her makeup and washing and drying her hands just for something constructive to do. Glancing at her watch, she saw that almost four minutes had passed since the bell. Even the worst stragglers would be safely at their desks by now.

Walking over to the door, she opened it a crack and peered out. The hallway was empty, and Callie heaved a sigh of relief. She stepped out and made her way toward her homeroom, her footsteps echoing on the tile floor. Just thirty yards now and she would be safe in the classroom.

One foot in front of the other, she told herself, walking forward steadily. *Get past Mr. Carpenter's room, then the boys' bathroom, then the language lab, and you're there.* Twenty-five yards. Twenty yards. Fifteen—

She almost screamed when George stepped out of

the boys' bathroom right in front of her. "Hi, Callie," he said with a broad smile.

Once again, she took off without even realizing she was doing it. Her shoes slipped on the smooth floor and she almost fell, but she managed to regain her balance and skidded the last few steps to the open door of her homeroom. She flung herself through, almost crashing into her teacher, who was standing just inside the door.

"Miss Forester!" Ms. Rourke said, clearly startled at her sudden entrance. "So nice of you to join us."

The rest of the class tittered. Callie ignored the laughter and glanced over her shoulder. She was half expecting George to follow her right into the classroom and start babbling at her. But there was no sign of him in the hall outside the doorway. Callie turned back to face the teacher.

"S-Sorry," she stammered as she met Ms. Rourke's disapproving gaze.

"Take your seat, Callie," the teacher said, turning and heading for her desk. "And please don't let it happen again."

Callie nodded and collapsed into her seat in the front row, relieved to have escaped with a warning. At least her luck hadn't totally deserted her. She was safe—for the moment.

She glanced at the still-open door and froze.

George was gliding past in the hall outside, staring into the classroom. His gaze met Callie's and he smiled. Then he turned and continued on his way, disappearing a second later.

Callie gulped, then pasted an innocent expression on her face as the teacher shot her a suspicious look. It seemed that *safe* was a relative term.

NINE

As Carole approached the school building on Monday morning, she felt herself growing slower and more sluggish with every step, like a barn-sour horse heading away from home. Now that it was over, winter vacation seemed to have passed in the blink of an eye. The second semester of her junior year loomed ahead, stretching so far into the future that she could hardly stand it. Algebra, English, biology—what did she really care about those subjects, anyway? Why should she have to put up with months and months of boring lectures on topics she would never need to use, when she could be at the stable doing what she really loved?

With some effort, she forced herself to stop thinking about it. It was that kind of attitude that had gotten her in trouble the previous semester. She had a year and a half of high school to go, and she might as well just accept that and make the best of it.

Once inside the school, she headed straight for her homeroom. *At least I have this afternoon to look forward to,* she reminded herself as she slung her backpack under the desk and slumped down in her chair, ignoring the other students as they wandered around the room and laughed and called to each other. *I can't wait to help introduce Jinx and Maddie to their new home.*

Smiling with anticipation, she thought about everything she had planned for the two new horses. Madison would be easy—all Carole and the rest of the staff had to do was settle her in and then ride her regularly for a week or so to work out any hidden kinks she might have. With any luck, the lesson kids would be riding her before long.

Jinx was another story, of course. Carole knew that the only reason Max had agreed to take him was because of her, and she didn't intend to let him down. She and Ben had sketched out a basic training schedule over the weekend, and Carole couldn't wait to start putting it into action.

We'll probably need to give him a few days to settle in before we get into anything too major, she thought, picking aimlessly at the peeling corner of her desk. *But we can start working on some basic ground manners right away, like leading and grooming and stuff.*

She blinked, distracted by a loud snort of laughter from nearby. For some reason her classmates seemed rowdier than usual that day. Carole supposed it had something to do with being the first day back after vacation. Doing her best to tune out the noise, she returned her thoughts to Pine Hollow. Thinking about the plans for Jinx made her think about Ben. She was starting to realize that he was part of the reason she was so excited about her new project. He was still being his new, friendly self, though no one except Carole seemed to have noticed.

It will be nice to work together on this, she thought. *It's nice that we're finally becoming more like real friends. At least I think that's what's happening there.*

Thinking about Ben—how she felt about him, what he might feel about her—always made her head hurt a little, so Carole did her best to put it out of her mind. She would have plenty of time to figure out what, if anything, was going on with them while they retrained Jinx.

She was glancing forward to see if the teacher had arrived yet when she noticed a couple of girls she barely knew staring at her intently. When they saw her look their way, both of them broke out in giggles and quickly turned away.

Carole frowned. What was that all about?

Before she could figure it out, Tanner Finnegan

leaned over from his seat across the aisle. "So, Carole," he said with a smirk, "I hear you had something going with Cam Nelson over the break."

Carole gulped, a quick, surprising stab of pain shooting through her heart at the sound of Cam's name. "What—um, what do you mean?" As far as she could recall, Tanner Finnegan had never said more than two words to her in the five months he'd been sitting across from her in homeroom. Why was he suddenly so interested in her love life?

"I heard all about it from the guys on the team." Tanner wiggled his eyebrows suggestively and leaned closer. "They said you and Cam were hot and heavy. For a while, anyway."

Carole felt her cheeks turning red. "It was no big deal," she muttered, not sure what else to say. She certainly didn't feel like discussing the way Cam had stomped on her heart with Tanner—or anyone, for that matter.

"Oh yeah? I hear Cam has quite the track record when it comes to lovin' 'em and leavin' 'em." Tanner grinned evilly. "So did you at least get some lovin' before you got left, Hanson?"

Blushing furiously, Carole turned away and pretended to search through her backpack for something, hoping Tanner would get the hint. If nothing else, she'd hoped the fact that Cam went to a different school would protect her from just this sort of thing. She'd forgotten that he knew plenty of people at Carole's school through the sports teams he played on, which often competed against Willow Creek High.

The teacher came in a moment later, saving Carole from any further questioning. She sat back in her chair, ignoring the morning announcements. Doing her best to forget about Tanner and his obnoxious comments, she turned her thoughts back to Jinx.

As she headed for her first period class, she was still lost in thought. But halfway there, she started to notice that a lot of people seemed to be staring at her and giggling as she walked by. She glanced around, feeling strange. *What's going on?* she wondered. *Did Tanner and the other guys on the team tell the whole world that Cam and I broke up? Why would anyone even care?*

She frowned and turned the corner toward her classroom. A tall guy she didn't know stared at her with a goofy grin on his face, then turned to whisper something to a friend. Both of them burst out laughing.

Carole blushed, ducking her head to avoid any more curious looks. As she hurried into her biology classroom, she almost ran into Andrea Barry. Andrea was in Carole's biology class, even though she was only a sophomore. She also boarded her horse, Country Doctor, at Pine Hollow.

"Oh!" Andrea said with an uncertain smile. "Um, hi, Carole."

Carole grabbed her arm. She and Andrea had never been especially close, but Carole knew that the younger girl was a nice, honest person. "Andrea," she whispered, dragging her into the room, "what's the deal? I feel like everyone is staring at me."

Andrea looked uncomfortable. "Yeah," she said, glancing over Carole's head. "Um, I guess people are sort of talking about what happened. You know, with you and that cute basketball player from Arden."

"Cam," Carole said, the name feeling slightly bitter on her tongue. "Why would anyone care? People break up all the time."

Andrea shrugged. "I guess some of the guys saw him the other night." She shifted her weight from one foot to the other, looking as though she wished she were anywhere else. But she went on. "And he was with, you know, that new girl he started going out with right before Christmas. . . ."

Carole froze. New girlfriend? Right before Christmas? There had to be some mistake. "But Cam and I didn't split up until New Year's!" she blurted out.

"Yeah." Andrea shot her a sympathetic look. "I know. I guess he was sort of bragging about that.

Dating two girls at once. You know—guys can be total pigs sometimes."

Carole barely heard Andrea as she excused herself and hurried to her seat. She walked to her own seat, feeling numb all over. Cam had been cheating on her? She couldn't believe it. She wasn't sure which was worse—that he'd done it or that he'd told the whole town all about it.

It's worse that he did it, she decided quickly, anger flaring up and mixing with her humiliation. *Much worse. But it was also really low of him to tell everyone about it. It's like he wanted me to look like an idiot. No wonder everyone in school is laughing at me.*

She shook her head, feeling like the world's biggest fool. Why hadn't she seen what Cam was really like? She had trusted him, and he had totally used her. And then he'd told everyone in town about it.

Only a real snake would kiss and tell like that, she thought, clenching her fists under her desk. *Most guys wouldn't do that, even if they broke up with someone. Alex wouldn't do it to Lisa. And Ben—*

She blinked, startled that Ben's name had popped into her head. Still, it was true. As far as she knew, he had never told a soul about that kiss at the horse show back in the fall. He had more class than that. More than Cam.

It felt a little strange to be comparing Ben to

Cam—and having Ben come out ahead. For a while, Cam had seemed a wonderful answer to her confusion about Ben. Everything had seemed so clear. He loved her, he wanted to be with her, and that was that.

Except it hadn't worked out that way. And now it seemed that Ben had been the nice one all along. He hadn't told her any lies, he hadn't gone out of his way to hurt her. In fact, he'd been there ever since Cam had dumped her, like a true friend.

Or am I just kidding myself? Carole wondered, hardly noticing as the teacher came in and called for order. *Am I just building Ben up in my mind because I'm so upset about Cam and I need someone else to distract me?*

She wasn't sure how to answer that. The only thing she knew for sure was that she'd better keep a low profile at school until the gossip blew over.

Lisa's stomach was grumbling by the time lunch period came. She had skipped breakfast that morning, mostly because her mother had been in the kitchen hunched over a cup of coffee and Lisa hadn't particularly felt like rehashing her breakup with Alex for the umpteenth time. Or, rather, listening to her mother urge her to rehash it so that she could experience "emotional healing."

I swear, Mom is going to drive me nuts with this

gripe therapy business, she thought as she entered the cafeteria and glanced around for an empty seat. *If I come away from this with any emotional scars, it's not going to be from the breakup itself. It'll be from Mom's constant nagging about honoring the grieving process and feeling my own pain.*

"Lisa! Over here!"

Lisa saw Polly Giacomin waving at her from a nearby table, gesturing to the empty spot beside her. Lisa was a little surprised—last time she'd checked, she and Polly hadn't been all that close. Even though they'd both ridden regularly at Pine Hollow for years and were in the same grade at school, they'd just never seemed to find much in common. Still, there was no sign of any of the friends Lisa usually sat with, so with a shrug, she headed for Polly's table.

"Hi!" Polly said eagerly as she sat down. "So, Lisa, how are you doing?"

"Fine, I guess," Lisa said, dumping her sandwich and apple out of her lunch bag. "I mean, you know, as well as could be expected. It's kind of a bummer to be back here." She rolled her eyes and glanced around the crowded cafeteria. Even after half a day back at school, the carefree days of winter vacation already seemed years in the past.

"I hear you," Polly said with feeling, her brown eyes widening. She placed a hand on Lisa's arm. "It must be especially hard for you—you know, since you won't be able to spend that much time with, you know . . ."

Lisa glanced down at Polly's hand in surprise. "Huh?" she said. "Oh!" The meaning of Polly's comment suddenly became crystal clear.

Wow, gossip sure travels fast around here, she thought wryly. *I guess this means the word is out about me and Scott.*

She wasn't quite sure how to feel about that. It was strange to know that people were talking about the two of them, especially when Lisa herself still didn't know quite what to think of their new relationship. She and Scott had gone on a trail ride with Stevie and Phil the day before, and it had been really nice. But Lisa still wasn't sure where she wanted things to go. She liked Scott, and she loved being with him. But did she really want to jump into a new romance so soon after Alex? Or would it be better to take a break, spend more time with her friends, get mentally prepared for college? The more she thought about it, the less certain she was about what she wanted to do.

"So Lisa." Polly leaned forward eagerly. "I just have to say, Scott Forester is such a total hottie. So is he really as romantic as he looks like he would be?"

Lisa smiled politely, trying to figure out how to answer. *Where was all this interest when I was going out with Alex?* she wondered. *It's like now that I'm dating Scott, I suddenly popped up on everyone's social radar or something. It's amazing. He doesn't even go to this school, but everyone knows him. I guess that's what comes from being almost clinically social—not to mention having a dad who makes the evening news almost every night.*

Spotting her friend Gary Korman ambling across the room, Lisa smiled apologetically. "Oops, I think Gary wants me. I'll catch you later, okay, Polly?"

Gathering up her lunch, she made her escape. It was a relief to get away from Polly's eager questions. Still, Lisa knew her reprieve was only temporary. If Polly was curious about Lisa's new relationship with Scott, lots of other people would be, too. Scott and his family were probably the closest things Willow Creek had to celebrities, and that meant people paid attention to everything they did—and everything anyone connected with them did, too. Lisa supposed that was just something she was going to have to get used to if she wanted to be with Scott.

It wasn't until Stevie walked into her American history class later that day that she realized George Wheeler was in the same class. *Wow,* she thought. *Was he there all first semester? I guess I never really noticed him.*

She smiled as George looked up from his books

and spotted her. "Hey," she called to him. "What's up, George?"

"Hi," he replied shyly as several nearby students shot them both curious looks.

Stevie guessed her classmates were surprised at her friendly greeting. It was common practice for most people to ignore George completely, except for a few obnoxious guys like Spike Anderson and Trent Lafferty, who delighted in teasing him and calling him names whenever they got bored. Stevie grimaced, feeling a twinge of guilt for looking the other way all the times she'd witnessed that kind of teasing in the past. If she'd known then what a nice, generous guy George really was, maybe she would have spoken up and put a stop to it.

Still, there wasn't much she could do about that now. She took the seat in front of George, then twisted around to talk to him. "So I was thinking about maybe starting some jumping today after school," she said. "Are you going to be around? I could use some eyes on the ground."

"Sure," George said immediately. "That sounds fine. Maybe we can set up some grids and stuff to start, kind of see how she reacts. Then we can figure out where to go from there."

"Great idea." Stevie smiled eagerly. "Like I said before, it's been a while since Belle and I did any serious jumping. We need to get back in practice—both of us."

"That reminds me," George said. "I just heard about a jumper schooling show they're holding over at Mendenhall Stables at the end of next month. I was thinking that could be a good goal for you and Belle to aim for. That way you'd be able to get back in practice jumping in competition, so it wouldn't all be new when you're ready to enter your first event in the spring."

"That's a great idea!" Stevie exclaimed. "Perfect, in fact. Thanks, George!"

"Sure." George's cheeks turned slightly pink, and he looked pleased. "Anyway, I need to go home after school and change clothes. But I can meet you at the stable around three-thirty if you want."

"Sounds like a plan." Stevie grinned at him, then turned around as the teacher entered. She was already looking forward to that afternoon's session. It was nice to have someone helping her train. When she worked on dressage, she mostly did it alone, unless Phil was around or Denise had time to give her a lesson.

It's amazing, she thought. *I mean, all I really knew about George before this was from what Callie told me, which made me assume he was some kind of chronically annoying, needy mess. It's kind of cool to see that there's actually a sweet, interesting guy underneath that nerdy exterior. It's just too bad he didn't turn out to be the guy for Callie.*

She couldn't help feeling a little disloyal to Callie for her thoughts. But she also couldn't help the way she felt, and she felt herself liking George a lot.

Pulling out her textbook as Mr. Carpenter started lecturing, Stevie shrugged off the moment of guilt. *Callie will get over this sooner or later, and then everything will be fine,* she thought as she flipped the book open to the correct chapter. *But until that happens, I just hope being friends with her doesn't mean I can't be friends with George, too.*

TEN

"Hey, handsome," Callie greeted her horse breathlessly that afternoon. "How's it going, Scoob?"

The friendly Appaloosa snuffled at her, then returned his attention to his grain bucket. Callie gave him a pat, then quickly picked up his feet and ran her hands over his body, checking for any problems that might need her attention. The horse seemed fine, so Callie gave him a quick scratch on the withers and then glanced at her watch. She was feeling rushed. For one thing, she was due at her doctor's appointment in less than half an hour. Normally her regular checkups were something she dreaded, but that day she was almost looking forward to it. That was because of the second reason she was feeling rushed: She was trying to get in and out of the stable before she ran into George.

"Okay, Scooby Doo," she murmured, letting herself out of the stall and then reaching over the half door to give the horse one last pat. "See you later. I'll just go make sure they know to turn you out for a few hours this afternoon. Let you stretch those cute spotted legs of yours."

She headed down the aisle, keeping an eye out for George. She was surprised he hadn't turned up yet. All day at school, he had seemed to be in her face every time she turned around. That freaky incident outside the bathroom had been the first encounter, but it hadn't ended there. She must have seen him two dozen times that day all over the school. In the halls between classes. In front of her on the stairs going down to the cafeteria. In the lunch line just a few people ahead of her. And, of course, there was chemistry class. Luckily the teacher had switched them around to new lab partners for the semester, so she didn't have to sit next to George anymore. But she could have sworn she'd felt his eyes watching her through the entire class from his seat several rows behind her.

Was he always around that much and I just never really noticed it before? she wondered as she crossed the stable entryway. *Or am I just going nuts—seeing him everywhere I turn, whether he's there or not?*

She wasn't sure. Once upon a time she had prided herself on being one of the most rational and practical people she knew. The old Callie would have scoffed at the way the new Callie was behaving— like the bogeyman was waiting to jump out at her everywhere she turned. But lately the new Callie had been feeling pretty irrational most of the time, and she wasn't sure how to deal with it. Maybe she really was going crazy. Maybe obsessing over George was just a symptom and she didn't realize it because she was too far gone. If so, she hoped the men in the white coats would arrive soon. She wasn't sure she could take many more days like that one.

When she reached the stable office, Max was there with his feet propped up on the desk, talking on the phone. Hearing him say something about foundations and load-bearing walls, Callie guessed that he was talking to the contractor who would be handling the expansion of the stable. But she didn't think about it for long. Quickly scribbling a note about Scooby's schedule, she gave Max a wave and then rushed out again.

As she reached the main doors she almost ran right into Stevie, who was hurrying into the stable with her arms wrapped around herself.

"Brrrr!" Stevie exclaimed when she saw Callie. "It's freezing out there!"

Callie nodded, feeling anxious. The last thing she wanted was to get sucked into a lengthy conversation with Stevie. "Yep," she said succinctly. "Gotta go. Doctor."

"Oh!" Stevie nodded understandingly. "Good luck."

"Thanks." Relieved at her quick escape, Callie continued on her way. Scott was waiting for her at the edge of the parking area, and she quickly hopped in the car, shivering. Stevie was right—it *was* cold.

"Ready?" Scott asked, already putting the car into gear.

Callie nodded. She could feel her tense body relaxing slightly as her brother pulled down the driveway. "Ready," she told Scott.

Lisa stared at the history textbook on the kitchen table in front of her. She had read the same paragraph about seven times, and she still wasn't sure what it said. She was too distracted by her mother, who had been hovering around her like a fly over a manure pile.

"Are you okay, honey?" Mrs. Atwood asked, perching briefly on the chair across from Lisa. "Can I get you something to eat?"

Lisa sighed. This had been going on for days now, ever since the official breakup on New Year's Eve. Over the weekend, whenever Mrs. Atwood wasn't at work or asleep, she had been trying to force Lisa to open up and share all her innermost feelings of grief and rejection. The more Lisa tried to explain that she really wasn't feeling those things anymore, the less her mother seemed to believe her.

"I'm fine, Mom," Lisa said as patiently as she could, though her voice came out sounding a little sharp. "I just need to read this chapter for tomorrow."

"Well, all right." Mrs. Atwood looked dubiously at the book. "Just don't work too hard. That's no substitute for facing up to your feelings, you know."

Lisa gritted her teeth as her mother wandered out of the room. Not for the first time, she wondered if she should just give in and tell her mother that she was already seeing someone new. She had kept that news to herself so far, mostly because she was a little afraid too see Mrs. Atwood's reaction when she heard about Scott. The Foresters were important people in town, and that had always been the kind of thing her mother cared about a lot. Lisa didn't relish the thought of dealing with her mother's excitement, especially when her own feelings were so new and uncertain.

She'd probably call up Congressman and Mrs. Forester and insist they come over for dinner, she thought with a shudder, folding and unfolding one corner of the page in front of her. *Then if they came, she'd spend the whole evening pretending to know all the important people in the entire universe and generally trying to impress them with her social importance. Then she'd probably start dropping hints about what a wonderful mother-in-law she would be for their darling Scott. . . .*

She grimaced. Maybe that last part was an exaggeration, but just barely. In any case, Lisa wasn't sure she wanted to take any chances right then. Still, she realized as her mother returned to the room, it might make things a lot easier to just go ahead and tell her.

"Lisa, dear," Mrs. Atwood said somberly. "I just want you to know, what you're feeling isn't wrong or shameful. The only thing wrong about grieving a betrayed love is keeping it all inside. I know you made a lot of plans based on the idea that you and Alex would be together, and now that that's all changed you have to be feeling lost and hurt. Honey, you have to help others to help you—that's the first step toward a renewed inner peace."

Lisa took a deep breath, trying to conceal her annoyance. It wouldn't do any good to blow up at her mother. It would probably only convince her all the more that Lisa was in some kind of deep emotional pain. "I think I'll go over to Pine Hollow for a little while," she said blandly. "I can finish my homework after dinner."

"Oh, darling." Her mother gazed at her with a sorrowful expression. "Are you sure? Wouldn't you rather stay here and talk? That sort of avoidance mechanism isn't going to work forever, you know. Sooner or later you have to let someone help you."

Lisa rolled her eyes. So now Pine Hollow was an

"avoidance mechanism"? She guessed that one had come straight out of her mother's latest gripe therapy meeting. Her mother opened her mouth to go on, but at that moment the phone rang.

Saved by the bell, Lisa thought, hopping out of her seat and grabbing the extension on the wall near the refrigerator.

"Hello?" she said. "Atwood residence."

"Hey, Lisa," Scott's familiar voice came through the line, sounding warm and inviting. "What's up?"

"Hi!" Lisa glanced at her mother out of the corner of her eye. Mrs. Atwood didn't seem to be paying attention to the call. She was staring up into space, looking thoughtful and concerned.

Probably coming up with more psychobabble to fling at me until I'm beaten into submission, Lisa thought ruefully. *Either that or she's revving up to start complaining again about how Dad did her wrong. I guess she thinks that kind of thing will make me feel better about my own situation, but it really just makes me want to throttle her.*

She was so distracted that it took her a moment to realize that Scott was speaking. ". . . but we could meet after that."

"Huh?" Lisa said. "Oh. Sorry, I mean, I didn't catch that."

"I said, do you want to grab some dinner tomorrow night?" Scott said patiently. "I have a student government officers' meeting after school, and it might run kind of long since it's the first one of the semester, but we could meet after I get out. How about it?"

Lisa hesitated, suddenly flashing back to their last restaurant date. She hadn't had all that much fun watching Scott talk to everyone in town except her. Of course, things had gotten a lot better once they'd left. In fact, she'd had an awfully nice time saying goodnight in the front seat of his car. . . . "Okay," she said. "It's a date."

"Cool." Scott sounded pleased. "I'll swing by and pick you up around five-thirty, give or take."

"Okay. See you then."

Lisa hung up and turned to find her mother watching her quizzically. "Was that one of your friends?" she asked sympathetically. "I do hope you're talking to them about this, since you're obviously not talking to me. Of course, they don't have nearly the same perspective on this sort of thing and I—"

"I'm not going out with my friends," Lisa blurted out before she quite knew what she was saying. "I have a date. With a guy."

Mrs. Atwood blinked. "I see," she said carefully.

Lisa took a deep breath. Now that she'd started, she might as well tell her everything. If nothing else, it would get her mother off her back about Alex.

"Yes," she said. "I have a date. With Scott Forester. And not our first date, either. I've been out with him several times already, and we're really getting along great. So you see, you can stop worrying about my emotional scars and my avoidance mechanisms or whatever. I'm just fine."

She braced herself, ready for an onslaught of excited questions about Scott. Instead, her mother just shook her head sadly. "Oh, my," she said. "This is worse than I thought."

"Huh?" Lisa cocked her head in surprise. "What are you talking about? I thought you'd be thrilled I was seeing someone like Scott."

Mrs. Atwood sighed. "Don't you know you can trust me, Lisa?" she asked sadly. "I'm your mother. You don't need to put on a brave front for me. And you certainly don't need to make up stories. If you're not ready to open up to me yet, just say so."

Lisa threw her hands in the air. She couldn't believe it. Her mother was totally out of control, and there didn't seem to be anything she could do about it. "Forget it. Just forget it," she snapped. "I'm going to the stable. I'll be back for dinner." Slapping her history book shut, she hurried out of the room before her mother could answer.

ELEVEN
11

Carole glanced at her watch and then looked through the gaping main stable doorway, her stomach fluttering eagerly. "It's almost three-thirty," she told Ben, who was sweeping the entryway. "They should be here soon."

Ben nodded and joined her at the door. Even though he didn't say anything, Carole could tell he was just as excited as she was. His dark eyes gleamed with interest, and he kept shifting his weight from one foot to the other and checking his watch.

Carole leaned forward to peer toward the road. It was more difficult than usual to see, since there were a couple of large bulldozer-type machines parked at the edge of the driveway. The contractor Max had hired to work on the expansion wasn't wasting any time getting started. In fact, the workers were supposed to break ground the very next day.

Carole felt oddly wistful when she thought about that. Pine Hollow had been the same for so long—

it was weird to think that things would soon be changing. Of course, people and horses had come and gone over the years she'd been riding there. But that wasn't really the same. The expansion felt much more serious somehow.

She glanced at Ben, who was still standing beside her. "It's going to be strange around here," she commented.

Ben nodded. "I know." He lifted his chin and gazed toward the road. "Look. It's them."

Carole followed his gaze and saw Pine Hollow's truck trundle into the driveway with a two-horse trailer behind it. With that, all nostalgic thoughts of the past fled, and she had to restrain herself from hopping up and down with excitement. She and Ben walked out into the chilly winter wind and waited as the large vehicle made its way slowly toward them and parked near the door.

"They're here!" Red O'Malley, who seemed happy and relaxed after his brief honeymoon, climbed out of the cab and grinned. "Like it or not."

"Did you have any trouble loading them?" Carole asked anxiously.

Red shrugged. "Madison walked right on like a pro," he said. "Jinx . . . Well, let's just say he took some convincing." He winked. "It's just lucky for us that he's crazy about apples."

Max emerged from the stable. "What's everybody standing around here for?" he barked. "Let's get these horses unloaded."

Carole grinned at Ben. He smiled back. It was just like Max to act so gruff and businesslike at such an exciting moment. But they set about doing as he said.

Madison was just as easy to unload as she'd been to load. She backed placidly off the trailer, took a look around, and then followed Red calmly into the stable.

"She goes in the stall across from Talisman," Max called.

Red tossed him a thumbs-up as he continued walking, chatting easily with the mare. Carole glanced at Max. "Should we get Jinx out?"

Max raised one eyebrow. "Absolutely," he said. "He's your project, isn't he? So you'd better get started."

Carole wasn't sure, but she thought she saw the ghost of a smile playing around the corners of the stable owner's mouth. *Okay,* she thought, stepping toward the trailer. *So this is a test, huh?*

She stepped forward eagerly. "Ben?" she said.

Ben immediately joined her, standing back as she entered the trailer through the front escape hatch. Inside, Jinx was rolling his eyes nervously, his small ears flicking back and forth. Carole could tell he was on the verge of panicking.

"It's okay, little guy," she crooned in her most soothing tone. "Don't worry, we'll have you out of here in just a second." She glanced toward the rear of the trailer, wanting to tell Ben to remove the center divider so that the pony wouldn't have to back off. If he was as leery of loading and unloading as it sounded like he was, it would be a lot easier if they could turn him around and lead him off headfirst.

Ben was already moving into the empty side of the trailer, clucking softly to let Jinx know he was there. The pony snorted in alarm, but as Ben started murmuring to him, he calmed down and returned his attention to Carole. She smiled. *I guess great minds think alike,* she thought as Ben set about dismantling the divider that had separated Jinx and Maddie on the trip over. *I didn't even have to mention what I wanted to do—he already knew.*

It was kind of a weird feeling when she looked at it that way. But she didn't have time to examine it just then. She kept talking to Jinx, patting him and scratching him and generally keeping him distracted for the few minutes it took Ben to clear the divider out of the way. After that, she coaxed Jinx into turning around inside the metal trailer, which he did with only a couple of minor kicks at the walls. Finally he was stepping carefully off the back.

"Good job," Ben said quietly, watching her from outside.

"Thanks." Carole gave Jinx an approving pat. "See, he's not nearly as bad as every—" At that moment a breeze kicked up in the stable yard, sending a dried leaf fluttering past. Jinx snorted and leaped to one side as if the leaf were a mountain lion. Carole went with him automatically, talking to him soothingly as he shuddered and stomped his feet, his tail swishing. He tried to pull away a couple of times, but she remained firm, insisting that he pay attention to her and settle down. Finally he started to focus on her again, and she breathed a sigh of relief. That had been close. She would have to stay on her toes with this one.

She finally got Jinx calm enough to take a few steps forward again. That was when the pony spotted the bulldozers farther down the driveway. Letting out another loud snort, he pricked his ears toward them in alarm. "Watch out," Ben murmured, never taking his eyes off Jinx's face. "He's thinking about blowing up again."

Once again, Carole spoke calmly to the pony, meanwhile turning him in a circle to distract him from the horse-eating monsters by the driveway. Jinx danced nervously, craning his neck to keep an eye on the bulldozers as long as he could.

"You okay?" Ben asked quietly.

Carole nodded, never taking her eyes off the horse. "Just give us a minute," she murmured.

Ben nodded and headed over to close up the truck. Carole patiently worked with the pony, convincing him that the monsters wouldn't get him as long as he behaved himself.

Just when Jinx was starting to relax again and pay attention to her rather than the bulldozers, Carole heard a shriek from the direction of the main doors. A second later half a dozen members of the intermediate riding class poured out of the building and ran toward them.

"Wait!" Carole called in alarm, her voice lost among the cries of the excited junior-high kids. "Stop! You're going to scare him."

The younger girls didn't pay any attention to her. They swarmed around Jinx, reaching out to pat him all over. The pony backed up, snorting anxiously, and Carole glanced helplessly at Ben, who was hurrying over from the truck.

"It's okay, Jinxie," Carole said helplessly. "Guys!" she hissed at the girls, who were all babbling at the same time about how pretty Jinx was and how much they wanted to ride him. "Please!"

When Ben reached the crowd, he stopped short. "Hey," he called to Carole. "He's doing okay."

Carole blinked, realizing it was true. The pony was still shifting his weight and flicking his ears, but he wasn't trying to get away.

Amazing, she thought. *He's freaked out by a leaf, but*

he doesn't mind a whole herd of giggling girls pawing him. I guess he is meant to be a kids' school pony after all!

Still, Carole figured they shouldn't press their luck. "Yo!" she shouted, her voice firmer. This time several of the girls glanced at her, most of them seeming to notice she was there for the first time. "Listen up," Carole continued. "You need to back off and let me get Jinx settled. He's a little nervous, and we have to let him calm down before we call out the welcome party, okay?"

"But Carole!" Alexandra Foster whined, still patting Jinx on the withers. "We just want to see him."

Carole opened her mouth to repeat herself, but she didn't get the chance. "You heard her," Ben said in his gruffest voice, stepping forward and glaring at the younger kids. "Move it. Now."

That was all it took. Carole hid a smile as the girls backed off immediately, eyeing Ben warily as they made room for Carole and the pony to pass. Carole knew that most of the younger riders at Pine Hollow—and some of the older ones, for that matter—were a little scared of Ben. She shot him a grateful look as she urged Jinx forward.

It took quite a while to reach the pony's new stall. Jinx insisted on taking a good, long look at every new thing they passed, from the other horses to a stack of empty water buckets. But finally Carole was leading him into his new home in the quiet rear corner of the stable loop. She and Ben had bedded down Jinx's new stall before his arrival, and the pony stepped in carefully after Carole, snuffling at the water bucket before zeroing in on the pile of fresh hay in the corner.

"There you go, boy," Carole said, unsnapping the lead line and giving the pony a pat. He ignored her, munching contentedly on the hay. "I'll let you settle in to your new home. Then maybe we can have a nice grooming or something, okay?"

The horse barely bothered to flick an ear in her direction as Carole let herself out of the stall: She closed the mesh top of the door as well as the solid bottom, hoping that would dissuade the younger riders from pestering the newcomer too much.

She was planning to go and check on the new mare, then see if Max needed help cleaning out the trailer. But she hesitated outside Jinx's stall for a moment, watching him eat. "We're going to make a great team, Jinx," she whispered. "Just wait and see. We'll show everyone how great you can be."

As she turned away, she saw Ben walking toward her. She blushed, wondering if he'd heard her words. But she also couldn't help thinking that she and Ben were starting to feel like a pretty good team, too.

Stevie chucked a wad of manure toward the wheelbarrow standing outside the horse trailer.

"Score!" she cried as it landed right in the middle of the small pile already there.

She turned and glanced around for any spots she might have missed. The trailer seemed clean, so she hopped out and leaned her shovel against the wheelbarrow. She was just in time to see George pulling into the parking area in his mother's white car.

"Hey!" she called to him as he got out of the car and hurried toward her. She shook her watch arm at him. "You're late! Thanks to you, I got corralled into helping Carole scoop poop while I waited."

George looked worried. "I'm sorry," he began. "I had to stop on the way over, and—"

Stevie grinned. "George, George," she said, punching him lightly on the arm. "If you're going to be hanging out with me, you're going to have to learn to take some joshing."

"Oh." George looked slightly confused but relieved. "Anyway, sorry I'm late. Can I help you finish up?"

"Sure, if you insist." Stevie glanced at the trailer. "I'll even give you a choice. You can either put the divider back in and close up the trailer, or you can wheel this bad boy back to the manure pile." She gestured at the half-full wheelbarrow.

"I'll take this." George grabbed the wheelbarrow's handles. "Be right back."

"Okay," Stevie said agreeably. As he headed off

around the corner of the building, she hurried to put the trailer back together. She couldn't wait to get started on their jumping practice. She'd been thinking about it all afternoon. Even though she hadn't jumped much lately, she had always loved it. The one regret she'd had when she started focusing more on dressage was that she wouldn't have much opportunity to jump.

That's why this new eventing idea is so perfect, she reminded herself happily as she finished restoring the trailer's divider and hopped off the back. *It lets me do everything I love all in the same competition.*

She was just latching the trailer doors when George reappeared. He hurried forward to help her push in the last stubborn latch. "So, you were helping Carole, huh?" he said as they finished and stepped back. "That's nice."

"Uh-huh." Stevie brushed off her hands on her breeches. "You know how it goes around here. If you're just standing around, you get put to work." She grinned to let him know she wasn't really complaining. Pine Hollow was one of the more affordable stables in the area, and she knew that a big part of that was Max's policy that everyone who rode there had to help out with stable chores.

"Carole's here a lot, huh?" George commented.

"Sure," Stevie said. "I mean, she works here, you know?"

"I know. But you guys are all here a lot," George said shyly. "Um, you know, you and all your friends. Carole, Lisa, Callie—um, are they all here today?"

"Lisa got here a few minutes ago," Stevie said. "I think she's in helping Denise with something. And Callie—" She paused, suddenly realizing what George was really after. "Um, I don't—Oh! Wait a minute. I did see her earlier. She was rushing off to a doctor's appointment."

"Oh." George cleared his throat. "I guess she probably won't come back here today, then, huh?"

Stevie shrugged. "No idea," she replied, feeling a little sorry for George. He still seemed to have it bad for Callie, and that was a shame. If he could just move on, realize it wasn't going to happen, he'd probably be a lot better off. So would Callie, judging by the way she'd acted the other night at that restaurant. "Come on," she said, figuring the least she could do was try to distract him. "Should we go set up some ground poles before I get Belle ready?"

"Sure," George said distractedly. "Um, I just want to look in on Joy first. I'll be back in a minute."

"Okay," Stevie said, already turning to head for the doors. "I'll meet you in the ring."

A few minutes later, Stevie had just dragged the last pole into line and was stepping off the distance when George emerged from the building. Stevie waved.

"How's this look?" she called.

George didn't answer. Instead, he hurried toward her with an anxious look on his face. "Stevie, I'm really sorry," he said breathlessly. "I just realized I told Max I'd pick up some more of Joy's hoof supplement. I—I guess I forgot, and now she's all out. I have to go pick some up—I'm not sure how long it will take me." He grimaced apologetically. "Would you mind if we put this off for another time?"

"Oh." Stevie was disappointed, but what could she say? "Of course not. Um, Belle and I can just trot some poles today and then work on flatwork. Maybe Lisa can spot me over a few cross rails or something. Then we'll be ready for you the next time."

"Thanks." George looked relieved. "Thanks for understanding, Stevie."

"Sure." Stevie waved as he hurried toward his car. Then she sighed and headed inside to tack up Belle.

TWELVE
12

When Carole looked in on Jinx a little while later, the pony was pacing restlessly in his stall. "Hi, short stuff," she called to him softly. "What's the matter? Don't you like your new home?"

The pony rolled his eyes at her suspiciously and continued to pace. Carole sighed, her mind flashing to Maddie. She'd just passed the mare's stall, and she was dozing in the corner after having polished off most of her hay.

Oh, well, she thought, unlatching the stall door and grabbing the lead rope from the hook outside. *Nobody said this was going to be easy.*

"Come on, boy," she crooned as she clipped the rope to Jinx's halter. "Let's go for a little walk. Then tomorrow, if you're good, we'll let you hang out in the paddock for a while, okay?"

Jinx snorted and tossed his head, but he followed as she led him out. He lifted his feet high at each step, almost prancing as they walked down the aisle to the rear entrance. Once outside he calmed down a little, though he followed her so closely she was afraid he was going to step on her feet.

"Okay, I know the first thing we need to work on," Carole murmured, calmly correcting him, forcing him to walk at a more reasonable distance from her. "I guess nobody ever really taught you how to lead properly."

She continued to work on Jinx's leading manners as she walked the pony around the back paddock and up and down the path to the manure pile and a few small outbuildings. There wasn't usually much traffic in that part of the stable yard, which was just what she wanted. She and Jinx weren't too likely to run into any intermediate riders or other curious onlookers back there.

Just as she was thinking of heading back inside, Ben appeared from the direction of the equipment shed. He walked toward her slowly, clucking until he was sure that Jinx saw him. Then he raised a hand in greeting. "How's he doing?" he asked Carole, nodding to the pony.

"Whoa." Carole waited until Jinx had halted beside her before turning to smile at Ben. "Okay," she said. "We're just doing a little remedial leading practice. He doesn't really seem to mind it—in fact, I think he wants to do the right thing. He just never learned how. I was just about to take him in and give him a treat for being a good boy. Maybe try some grooming, too, to keep him from getting too lonely on his first day here."

Ben nodded thoughtfully. "Need help?"

"Sure, if you want!" Realizing she might have sounded a little overeager, Carole cleared her throat. "Er, I mean, that might be a good idea. A little extra attention might calm him down, and if both of us are there it will be easier to control him if he gets nervous. Right?" she added uncertainly, suddenly wondering if she was really thinking only of the pony's best interests at the moment. Or was it Carole herself who would be happier to have Ben there helping her?

Before she could make up her mind, Ben nodded. "Sounds good."

"Okay." Carole turned and led the way inside, taking deep breaths to get over the sudden attack of embarrassment. By the time they had the pony tied to the ring in the stall wall, she was feeling almost normal.

As Carole patted the pony, Ben went out to fetch the bucket of grooming tools Carole had left in the aisle earlier. Hanging it from one of the stall's safety hooks, he reached in and pulled out a hoof pick.

"Shall I?" he asked.

Carole nodded. "Careful, though. We never

picked up his feet the other day when we were looking at him—he could give you some trouble. I'll
stay by his head if you want." At Ben's nod, she
moved into position, scratching the pony and talking to him to distract him from what Ben was
doing.

To her surprise, Ben had little difficulty picking
up and cleaning Jinx's hooves. The pony balked
slightly when he ran his hand down his left fore, and
he made a halfhearted kick with his left hind leg
when Ben touched it. After that, though, he stood
quietly and allowed the young stable hand to do
whatever he wanted with his right feet.

Wow, Carole thought as she watched. *I always
forget just how great he is with horses—how they seem
to trust him so totally.*

"There," Ben said as he finished his task. He
stood and dropped the pick back in the bucket,
brushing off his hands. "Not too bad."

"Not too bad at all," Carole agreed, patting the
pony proudly. She started toward the bucket to grab
a brush. Her hand reached out at the same time as
Ben's, and she felt her fingernails scrape the back of
his hand. "Oops!" she said, blushing. "Sorry about
that."

"S'okay," Ben mumbled quickly, pulling out a
body brush and turning away. Without another
word, he started working on Jinx's right side.

Were his cheeks turning slightly red, too? Carole wasn't sure, but she couldn't help feeling flustered about the close encounter. She took a deep breath, trying not to think about it. *We're here to groom a horse,* she told herself firmly. *That's all. No biggie.*

Deciding she'd better get to it, she grabbed a brush and moved around to the pony's left side, across from Ben. Soon she found her thoughts wandering as she moved the brush steadily over Jinx's body. As it so often did lately, her mind turned first to Cam. She realized that hearing at school that day about what a rat her ex-boyfriend really was actually made things a little clearer. A day ago, despite Cam's despicable behavior on New Year's Eve, she still might have forgiven him if he'd come crawling back. She might have believed him if he'd apologized. After discovering just how deceitful he'd really been, though, she was finally starting to understand that she was better off without him. It still hurt to think about how she'd loved him. It hurt a lot. But the pain subsided a little bit when she was with Ben. Being with him reminded her that some guys really were decent and honest.

Maybe Ben's not perfect, she thought, glancing at him as he bent to brush some dried mud off Jinx's fetlock. *But he doesn't pretend to be anything he's not. The horses would know if he were a fake, and they all totally love him and trust him. I suppose that should be telling me something. . . .*

She shook her head, banishing the thought immediately. All she knew was that she was happy to be there with Ben at that moment, doing what they both loved. She didn't want to think too far beyond that.

As she picked at a crusty spot of dirt on Jinx's rump, the pony suddenly flicked his tail, catching her square across the face. "Ow!" she yelped, jumping back. The stinging sensation faded quickly from her face but remained in her left eye. She rubbed it, but that only made the pain worse.

"You okay?" Ben asked, peering around Jinx's head.

Carole blinked and squinted, trying to get a few tears going to wash out her irritated eye. "He just got me with his tail," she said. "I think some dirt or something got in my eye."

"Let me see." Ben left the pony and stepped over to her, gazing into her face with concern.

Carole gulped. He was standing so close that she caught a faint whiff of aftershave mixed with the more familiar scent of horses. "Um, it's this one," she mumbled nervously, pointing to her left eye.

"Hold still," Ben commanded gruffly, leaning closer. Carole held her breath as he stared into her eye. Suddenly she flashed back to that day more than a month earlier at the horse show, when the two of them had been just this close. Carole had been trying to forget about their one and only kiss almost since it had happened. But now it all came rushing back, filling her mind. For an instant she was afraid she might grab him and kiss him now. But she didn't, and the strange, intense moment lingered endlessly, with neither of them moving a muscle as they stared at each other.

Finally Ben cleared his throat and backed away a few steps. "Er, it's too dark in here." He glanced at the overhead bulb, which cast a dull yellowish glow over the stall. "Better go outside where we can see."

"Okay." Carole felt an odd flash of disappointment as she followed him out of the stall. The flow of air made her injured eye sting more, so she put one hand over it. Halfway to the back door, she almost tripped over a lead rope someone had left lying in the aisle.

"Watch it." Ben grabbed her elbow to steady her. "Here. This way."

Carole tried to remember to breathe as he steered her. She was very aware of his hand on her arm, even through her thick sweatshirt. And she couldn't help noticing that he didn't remove his hand even after they had negotiated past the tricky lead rope.

She also couldn't help being glad about that.

Callie was feeling pretty good as she emerged from the medical building on Catalpa Street. She stepped onto the sidewalk outside and blinked, allowing her eyes to adjust to the garish pink-and-orange glow of the winter sun as it sank toward the western horizon. It was a little after five, and people were hurrying along the sidewalks, newly released from the businesses up and down the block. Cars were whizzing by in both directions, and across the street a couple of little boys were chasing each other up and down the stoop in front of a shoe repair shop.

Callie felt the energy of all the activity surrounding her surge through her as she lingered on the sidewalk for another moment or two. She couldn't wait to tell her parents what the doctor had said that day. After more than six long months, he had finally told Callie that her legs were back to being as strong and healthy as they'd ever been. All her hard work in physical therapy had paid off, and she could finally put the accident behind her, once and for all, and move on with her life.

I'm back on my feet, one hundred percent sound at last, she thought, taking a deep breath of the chilly evening air. *I have a great horse to work with. That means the only thing standing in my way is myself. Not George—me. And that's something I'm just going to have to deal with. I've been holding myself back long enough.*

She glanced at her watch, hoping that Scott hadn't grown too impatient while waiting to drive her home. The doctor had been running a little behind schedule, as usual, and Callie had spent most of her twenty-five minutes in the waiting room pondering her life, past and future, and what she was going to do about it. One thing she had figured out for sure: She couldn't afford to waste any more time skulking around, worrying every second about George Wheeler.

I have to talk to George one more time, she thought firmly as she stepped off toward the bookstore at the other end of the block, where Scott was waiting for her. *And this time, I have to make sure he understands me clearly. I just let things get too far out of hand before, that's all. This time I'll confront him straight on, ask him what the deal is and then tell him he has to stay away from me from now on. Period. End of story.*

She smiled slightly, feeling a little better now that she had a plan. As she stepped around a portly woman talking on a cell phone, the smile froze on her face: George was walking toward her from just a few yards away.

She stopped short, her head spinning. *No!* she thought helplessly. *No! He can't be here now. No!*

"Hi, Callie!" George exclaimed, his face splitting

into a broad grin. "What a coincidence! What are you doing here?"

She just stared at him for a moment, frozen with shock. No. This was too sudden, too unexpected and unnerving. She couldn't face him now, like this. No.

Her legs took off before her mind even managed to send the message. She sprinted, hardly noticing which way she was going.

"Callie, wait!"

She heard his footsteps pounding after her. But she outran him easily, dodging around startled people on the sidewalk and finally ducking down a narrow alley between a print shop and an insurance office. She slipped behind a large trash bin, peering out until she saw George wander by, looking disappointed and confused.

She relaxed and leaned back against the cold, hard surface of the trash bin. As she moved her foot slightly, she heard something squish.

"Oh, gross," she murmured as she realized she'd just put her foot in something brown and slimy—obviously, someone in the Chinese restaurant next door had missed the bin. Standing up, she did her best to scrape the gooey mess off her shoe. Then she collapsed back against the brick wall of the building behind her, checking first to make sure it was relatively clean.

Is this what it's come to? she wondered helplessly, shivering slightly as a cold wind swept through the alley. *Is this really what my life has become? Sneaking around, running away, lying to my family and friends, hiding in the garbage behind restaurants?*

She squeezed her eyes shut, wishing she could go back in time and change her own behavior. Make different choices, take different steps early on to prevent all this from happening. But would that really have worked?

No, she realized, the truth suddenly dawning on her as if it had been there all along. *No, I guess it probably wouldn't. Sure, maybe I could've been more honest with George in the beginning. But that doesn't mean I caused this. There are plenty of other guys who get rejected and don't end up acting this way.*

She opened her eyes and blinked, wondering why she'd never seen it in that light before. Why had she been so quick to blame herself? What had kept her from seeing that this was George's problem, not hers? He was the one who was behaving inappropriately—and no matter how she tried to rationalize or ignore them, the things he'd been doing *were* inappropriate. Following her into the woods. Peeking in her window. Yes, even talking to her and trying to hang out with her when she'd specifically asked him not to. It was wrong of him to do these things. Not her—*him.* So why hadn't she realized that until now?

I guess ruining my favorite pair of shoes was the straw that broke the camel's back, she thought wryly, glancing down at the gloppy stain on the brown leather of her left toe. But she didn't really care about her shoe. For the first time in a long time, she felt certain about what she needed to do, and she knew that she could do it. *It's way past time to do what I was thinking about before,* she told herself firmly, already heading out toward the sidewalk. *I've got to tell George that this is over. For good. And this time I'll make sure he knows I mean it.*

"Good girl," Stevie crooned, feeding her horse a carrot. "You did great today, sweetie!"

Belle chewed the carrot quickly and snuffled at Stevie's hands, clearly hoping for more. When she realized it was all gone, the sleek, long-legged bay mare lowered her head to check the ground for any stray pieces.

Stevie grinned and tugged at the lead rope. "Come on, piggie," she said, reaching out to adjust Belle's anti-sweat sheet. "Keep moving. As soon as we get you cooled out, you can oink your way through all the hay in your stall."

They circled the stable building several times. As they walked, Stevie thought about their training session. It had gone pretty well. After warming up, she had worked over the ground poles for a while. Then

Lisa had hung around for a few minutes to watch as Stevie took Belle over a couple of lines of cross rails. Belle had performed well, proving that she hadn't forgotten all her previous jump training. Still, Stevie knew that they hadn't accomplished nearly as much as they would have if George had been there coaching her.

I hope George isn't going to flake out on me now, she thought. *I really need his help if I'm going to be ready for that jumper show next month. I mean, where else am I going to get free lessons between now and then?*

She rolled her eyes at that, feeling slightly guilty. Just because George had needed to run an errand for his own horse that day, it didn't mean he was blowing her off. He seemed downright eager to help, in fact. She should be grateful.

And I totally am, she reminded herself. *It's great that he came along to help me with this, especially when I never would have expected it. He's just not the kind of guy I ever thought I'd be—*

She stopped short as she rounded the corner, all thoughts of George and eventing fleeing immediately as she spotted Carole and Ben. The two of them had just emerged from the stable's rear exit. Ben had his hand on Carole's arm, steering her as she held one hand over her left eye.

"There," Ben said, his words carrying to Stevie

through the cold, still, late-afternoon air. "Better. Now maybe we can see—"

As Stevie watched, Carole tipped her head back and removed her hand. Ben moved closer, his face only inches from hers as he peered into her eye. His free hand hovered near her cheek. Both of them were clearly unaware that they were being observed.

What the heck is going on here? Stevie wondered. One answer to that question was obvious: Carole had something in her eye and Ben was helping her get if out. But that wasn't the part that was worrying her. If the person helping Carole had been Lisa or Red or just about anyone else at Pine Hollow, Stevie wouldn't have given it a second thought. But since when had Ben turned into Mr. Helpful? And did he really have to stand so close, or keep his hand on Carole's arm as he peered into her eye? For that matter, did Carole have to gaze back up at him with that trusting, vulnerable expression on her face? Stevie could almost see the sparks flying between them, and she didn't like it. Not one bit.

This could be really bad for Carole, she thought grimly as she watched them. *First she gets blown away by the whole Cam thing. And now? Well, let's just say Ben isn't exactly Mr. Sensitive. If she starts to fall for him again and he hurts her . . .*

Finally, as Ben gently touched the skin just under

Carole's eye, Stevie couldn't stand it any longer. "Hey!" she called loudly. "Need some help?"

Carole and Ben both jumped, Ben almost poking Carole in the eye as they leaped apart. Stevie hurried forward with Belle in tow.

"S-Stevie!" Carole blurted out, blushing and looking sheepish.

That was all Stevie needed to see. *Didn't she learn anything from the whole Cam fiasco?* she thought, feeling almost angry at her friend. *Is she really that naive? I mean, I can see how Cam fooled her—he was a real pro, he fooled all of us. But anyone who's ever met Ben Marlow can see that he's just a heartbreak waiting to happen.*

She cast a disgruntled glance at Ben. Yes, he was good-looking. Stevie would be the first to admit that. But he was so gruff and sullen, so obsessively private—he was almost guaranteed to hurt Carole if she let herself start believing she could have a relationship with him like the one she'd had—or thought she'd had, anyway—with Cam.

"Got something in your eye, Carole?" Stevie did her best to hide her thoughts as she pushed past Ben to peer into Carole's eye herself, Belle still trailing along at the end of her lead rope. She must have shoved Ben a little too hard, though, because he scowled at her darkly before turning away.

"Um, yeah." Carole glanced helplessly from Stevie to Ben and back again, making it impossible for Stevie to spot any foreign objects in her dark brown eyes.

"Hold still," she commanded sternly.

Ben was already moving away toward the stable door. "Ben," Carole called, her voice so uncertain and raw that it made Stevie cringe.

He glanced back at her briefly, his eyes hooded and almost hostile. "Gotta go," he said shortly.

Stevie waited until he'd disappeared inside, then rounded on Carole. "What's the deal?" she hissed. "You and Ben were looking awfully friendly there. I thought you decided that kind of thing was a bad idea. So what's up with that?"

Carole frowned. "It's not how you think," she said, sounding defensive. "You don't know him like I do. Besides, it's not like anything—"

"There you are!" Maureen's loud voice interrupted. The stable hand emerged from the building and walked toward them. "Stevie, I've been looking all over for Belle. You wanted the farrier to look at her, right?"

"Oh!" Stevie had completely forgotten about that. "Sorry, Maureen. I'm coming right now."

She turned back to her friend, planning to insist on talking to her more after she finished with the farrier. But Carole was already hurrying back toward the stable.

"Carole, wait!" Stevie called, wondering if she'd been too harsh. Carole could be so sensitive when it came to guys. Maybe she should have taken it a little easier on her. She had just been so surprised to come upon her and Ben like that, especially so soon after that bad scene with Cam.

Carole paused, though she didn't meet Stevie's eye. "I've got to go wash my eye out," she mumbled. "See you later."

She hurried away before Stevie could respond. Stevie hesitated, then turned and clucked to Belle, leading her after Maureen. She would have to find out what was going on with Carole later.

THIRTEEN

The next afternoon Callie picked at a stubborn spot of dried mud on Scooby's flank. Scooby snorted in alarm and shifted his weight, trying to get away from her probing fingers. "It's okay, boy," Callie murmured soothingly. The Appaloosa had been uncharacteristically jumpy ever since she'd started grooming him that day, and she was pretty sure she knew why.

He's probably picking up on my nerves, she thought ruefully. *He can tell I'm all freaked out today, and it's making him anxious. Sort of the way running into George Wheeler every time I turn around has been making me anxious.*

She grimaced slightly, wishing she could just find a private moment to have it out with him. The more she put off their final conversation, the worse he was going to get—she had already encountered him several times since arriving at Pine Hollow an hour earlier.

And each time it's a huge coincidence, she thought sarcastically, glancing into the aisle as Ruffian, one of the stable cats, slunk past Scooby's stall. *Yeah, right. The same way it's a coincidence when Ruffian just happens to end up with a mouse in her teeth.*

She sighed and tossed her currycomb into her grooming kit. She wasn't accomplishing much with Scooby at the moment—she might as well leave him in peace. She was basically marking time anyway. She knew that George was exercising Joyride in the indoor ring, and she intended to be waiting for him when he was finished. She was sick of being nervous all the time. She hated feeling as though she had to check over her shoulder every five minutes, to skulk around like an escaped convict at Pine Hollow, at school, on the street, and even in her own home. She felt like a fool for letting herself reach that point. After all, it was *George Wheeler* she was dealing with. He was so dorky, so ridiculously harmless and bumbling. How could she have allowed herself to become so frightened of someone like him? It just didn't make sense, any more than it made sense to blame herself for George's weird, pathetic behavior. It was just one more reason it had to end then and there.

Taking a deep breath, she let herself out of Scooby's stall and walked around to the opposite end of the stable aisle, where Joyride was kept. The stall was still empty, which meant that George and the mare hadn't finished their workout yet. Callie took advantage of the wait to prepare herself for the coming confrontation, running over what she wanted to say in her mind.

Finally she heard the clip-clop of hoofbeats crossing the entryway. A moment later George appeared with Joyride at his shoulder. The mare snorted suspiciously when she spotted Callie, but George broke out in a delighted grin.

"Hi, Callie!" he said, tugging on his mare's reins to move her along faster. "What are you doing here?"

"Waiting for you," Callie replied grimly, not returning his smile. "George, we need to talk."

"Sure thing, Callie." George's gray eyes were wide and benign. "Just give me a second to untack Joy. Unless you want to talk while I work?"

"That's okay. I'll wait." Callie crossed her arms over her chest and did just that as George led his horse into her stall and quickly removed her bridle and saddle. He dumped the saddle on the ground outside and slung the bridle over the edge of the door. Then he blinked at Callie expectantly as he removed his hard hat and set it aside.

"Okay, what is it, Callie?" George asked.

Instead of answering, Callie crooked her finger, gesturing for him to follow as she led the way to the empty stall at the very end of the row, beside the back door. She didn't want any spectators, and she definitely didn't want to be interrupted. It was time to have it out with George once and for all, and she was determined not to let anything stop her.

He followed her into the clean-swept stall obediently, almost stumbling over a couple of bags of sweet feed someone had stored there. "What's going on, Callie?" he asked anxiously. "Are you—"

"Quiet," she interrupted bluntly, turning to face him. "Listen to me, George. I have a few things to say to you, and I want you to really hear them this time."

George cocked his head to one side. "What do you—"

"Wait," she commanded, holding up one hand. "It's not your turn to talk yet. It's your turn to listen."

George gulped, looking startled. But he nodded meekly.

Callie tilted her chin slightly, willing herself to be strong and firm. "I know you've been following me around lately," she said. "And I want you to know, I'm on to you. And I'm sick and tired of it. Do you hear me?"

"But Callie—"

"Shut up!" she shouted, louder than she'd intended. She cleared her throat. "You're still listening," she said sternly. "And I'm telling you, I'm fed up. I won't take it anymore. From this point on, you need to stop it. I don't want any more 'coincidental' meetings in the schooling ring, or in town, or in the halls between classes, or out on the trails where I'm training. And I absolutely don't want to see you anywhere near my house again."

George looked startled and opened his mouth. Callie cut him off before he could make a sound.

"Yes, I saw you through the window that night," she snapped. "So don't bother to deny it. I've had enough of that, and of you. I don't want to *see* you, I don't want to *talk* to you, I don't want to know you *exist*. And you're the one who's going to make that happen, whether you like it or not. I don't know what kind of relationship you think we have, or ought to have, in your pathetic little mind, but I'm putting an end to it. For good. No more excuses."

George's jaw had dropped during her speech, giving him the appearance of a wounded puppy. Finally he snapped his mouth closed and shifted his gaze to somewhere just north of her right shoulder. "Is that all?" he asked quietly.

"Almost," she said. "We've had this conversation before, you and I. This time I want you to know I'm serious. I want you to tell me you understand what the deal is. If I catch you at it again, there's going to be hell to pay." She made her expression as fierce as she could at that last part, hoping he would get the hint.

George didn't reply, but he nodded, looking a little shell-shocked. "I—I'd better go now," he mumbled. Without another word, he hurried past her and out of the stall. By the time she stepped into the aisle herself, he'd disappeared.

Good, she thought with relief. *Finally. That's over with.*

A huge weight had lifted off her heart and mind at the very moment George had slunk out of the stall. Callie was finally free. She could get back to her life now.

Turning toward Scooby's stall, she walked forward with a spring in her step. Suddenly she felt like going for a nice long trail ride.

Lisa was still thinking about the photography club meeting she'd just left as she pulled out her keys to let herself into her house. To her surprise, however, she found that the door was already unlocked.

That's weird, she thought as she pushed it open. *I thought Mom was working tonight.*

She felt a twinge of worry. Her mother's attendance record at the clothing store where she worked hadn't been too stellar lately. Lisa hoped she hadn't decided to take another random day off. If she kept it up, she was going to be hitting the unemployment office soon.

"Mom?" Lisa called as she stepped inside and dropped her backpack on the chair near the door. "Are you home?"

"In here!" Mrs. Atwood's voice, sounding oddly muffled, called from the direction of the kitchen.

Lisa shrugged off her coat and walked down the hall. It was already growing dark inside the house—that time of year, dusk came early—but there were no lights on in the kitchen.

Uh-oh, Lisa thought uneasily. *I hope Mom's not sitting in there in the dark.* She still hated thinking about the difficult days right after her parents' divorce, when her mother had spent most of her time locked in her bedroom with the lights off, drinking wine and crying nonstop.

"Mom?" Lisa said tentatively as she turned the corner into the kitchen. She reached for the light switch by the door. "Are you—"

"Surprise!" Mrs. Atwood cried as the light came on, illuminating their very crowded-looking kitchen. Six people were seated at the kitchen table, while another four or five were clustered around the island counter. Mrs. Atwood stepped forward and took Lisa's hand. "Come in, Lisa. Sit down!"

Lisa shook her head, completely confused. "What's going on?" she asked. "Who are all these people?"

"They're here to help you, darling." Mrs. Atwood smiled and tugged at her again. "They're just a few people from my group who want to let you know it's okay to share your feelings."

"What?" Lisa gaped at the strangers in her kitchen, feeling very unreal. This couldn't actually be happening, could it? Even her mother wasn't crazy enough to drag her entire therapy group out to their home. "But I told you, Mom!" she said. "I'm fine! There's really nothing to share."

"Come, Lisa," said a tall, thin man with several strands of grayish hair combed over his otherwise bald head. He stood from his seat at the table and gestured to her. "Take my seat. We're here to help, just as your mother said."

"That's right." This time a portly woman dressed in leopard-print stirrup pants spoke up. "We're here to support you, Lisa. After what you've been through, you need a soft cushion of caring to fall upon."

"What I've been through?" Lisa said, glancing at her mother in horror. "What have you been telling these people about me, Mom?"

Mrs. Atwood shrugged and waved her hands

vaguely. "Don't be upset, Lisa," she said. "I just told them about your loss. I'm your mother, after all—whether you know it or not, your pain affects me deeply. That causes me pain. Naturally, I shared that with my friends here, and they just insisted that we had to do something to help you."

Lisa gritted her teeth. This whole scene was starting to feel like some kind of bad made-for-TV movie. What was her mother's problem, anyway? It was bad enough that she had spent the past week pestering Lisa nonstop. Did she really have to bring in reinforcements to make things even more unbearable?

"Your mother also told us that you were keeping your feelings bottled," a petite, earnest-looking red-haired woman said. "Letting rejection and resentfulness build up inside you without sharing them is terribly unhealthy. So when she asked us for help, well, of course we came right away."

The leopard-print woman nodded vigorously. "You don't have to be ashamed to share your pain with us, dear. I didn't have the best track record with men, either," she confided with an exaggerated wink. "That is, not until I met my Marvin." She grasped the comb-over man's hand and squeezed it to her sizable bosom.

Marvin leaned over to kiss her on the cheek.

Then he blinked at Lisa with sympathetic brown eyes. "We can help you," he said fervently. "You just have to let us."

"Okay, listen, Mom," Lisa said grimly, ignoring the others. "I know you're having trouble believing this, but I really don't need any emotional healing right now. Alex and I are better off apart—we've both accepted that, and we're both moving on. Like I told you, I'm already dating Scott Forester."

"Forester?" a woman near the back of the room said. "Is that the senator's son you were talking about, Eleanor?"

"Yes, I'm afraid so," Mrs. Atwood replied, still gazing at Lisa sorrowfully. "He's an acquaintance of Lisa's, but I'm afraid she's made him out to be a bit more lately, as I was telling you at the last meeting."

"He's a congressman's son," Lisa snapped, fed up with the whole ridiculous scene. "I've been dating him since before Christmas. He's crazy about me, and I think he's totally amazing. He's a fantastic kisser, and every time he touches me, it makes me tingle all over. Oh yeah, and we have a date tonight. There. Enough sharing for you, Mom?"

She crossed her arms over her chest, waiting for her mother to purse her lips in dismay and say something about not being so crude in front of company. But once again, Mrs. Atwood just shook her head sadly. "If you say so, dear," she said. "But really, wouldn't it be easier in the long run if you just faced things now instead of hiding behind a false front?"

"Aargh!" Lisa threw her hands in the air. She couldn't take it anymore. Before her mother could stop her, she whirled and stomped out of the room. Pausing just long enough to grab her coat and keys, she headed outside. It was still a little early, but she headed for the Foresters' house to meet Scott. Suddenly she couldn't wait to start their date.

"Wow," Callie commented aloud as she glanced at her watch, though the only one around to hear her was Scooby. "It's later than I thought."

Scooby had made a beeline for his grain bucket as soon as she'd led him into his stall, and he didn't respond. Callie smiled at him, amazed at her own luck in finding such a wonderful horse. Scooby had performed like a dream out on the trail that afternoon, crossing streams and scrambling up steep banks as easily as most horses walked across a paddock. It had been really nice to ride without worrying about anything more troubling than whether Scooby was breathing hard or the girth was coming loose. Finally having it out with George had given her such a feeling of freedom, Callie had been tempted to keep riding all night. Only the dark had chased her back in. She had been farther from Pine

Hollow than she'd realized, and by the time they reached the broad fields beyond the stable, she had been relying on Scooby's superior night vision to guide them through the darkness.

"But we made it back safe and sound, didn't we?" she whispered into the horse's ear, glad that she'd taken the extra time to hand walk him until he was completely cooled out. "We make a good team."

Since Scooby was still far more interested in his late dinner than in her compliments, Callie gave him a pat and left him alone to finish eating. She could come back after she'd put his tack away and give him a quick grooming. Now that she had her freedom back, she didn't want to leave the stable. She'd been stuck at home for too long.

In the tack room, Callie hummed to herself as she slung her saddle onto its assigned rack, then wiped off her bit and hung up the bridle. Checking her watch again, she saw that it was almost ten o'clock. She wondered if she should call home and let her parents know where she was. Then she remembered that they were out at a dinner for the other members of her father's welfare committee—they probably weren't even home yet.

Good, she thought with satisfaction. *Then I don't have to hurry.*

She walked across the hall to the girls' bathroom. As she washed her hands, she found herself staring at the reflection in the mirror of the room's single high, narrow window. Unless she missed her guess, it would give her a clear view right across the stable yard to the parking lot beyond.

So what? she thought, a little annoyed with herself. *My plan worked. He's not here. I would have seen him by now. Probably about fifty times already.*

Still, she couldn't resist. Drying her hands on a paper towel, she turned and walked over to the window. She crumpled the damp towel, winged it over her shoulder at the trash, and then stood on tiptoes to grab the edge of the window. Pulling herself up, she was just able to peer over the sill. Sure enough, the parking lot was clearly visible, illuminated by the stable's safety spotlight, which stayed on all the time. Callie could see that the only vehicle parked there was the stable's battered old truck, still hitched to the horse trailer that had brought the two new horses over the day before.

Smiling with relief, Callie let go of the window. *See?* she chided herself. *No white car. No problem.*

The windowsill had been dusty, so she rinsed her hands again quickly. Then she hurried out of the room, humming softly again under her breath. Stopping by the tack room just long enough to grab her grooming kit, she headed back toward Scooby's stall.

"Finished eating, Scoob?" she sang out as she approached. "I hope so, because I—"

She gasped, all the breath leaving her body as she swung open the stall door. Scooby seemed to be finished with his grain. He was standing calmly in the middle of the stall. At his side, feeding him something from his hand, was George Wheeler.

"Hi, Callie," George said in his bland, high-pitched voice. "What a coincidence seeing you here."

Callie's head spun. All she could do was open her mouth and try to scream, but nothing came out.

FOURTEEN
14

Carole blinked and frowned, pausing in the act of stacking rubber bell boots on a shelf. "Did you hear something?" she commented.

Ben glanced at the door of the equipment shed, which was closed tight against the frigid evening air. "Nope," he said, returning his attention to the sheet of paper in front of him. He made a check mark on it with a stubby pencil, then stood to return half a case of leather conditioner to its assigned shelf. "Probably the wind."

"Oh. You're probably right." Carole shrugged. "Anyway, it definitely didn't sound like a horse."

Ben nodded his agreement and resumed his seat on an overturned bucket. Carole smiled, glad that that was settled. The last thing she felt like doing at that moment was leaving the cozy shed to go investigate strange noises in the night. She and Ben had been working together for the past hour or two, taking inventory of the shed. They had spent the first few minutes discussing Jinx and his training, then lapsed into a companionable silence broken only by the occasional question or comment about the contents of the floor-to-ceiling shelves. Carole had been pleasantly surprised when Ben had offered to stay and help with the inventory—it meant putting in extra hours, and Ben spent an awful lot of hours at the stable as it was. But thanks to their hard work, the overstuffed shed was almost completely organized and inventoried. There were only two shelves to go, and Carole was a little disappointed that they would be finished soon.

This is nice, she thought, not for the first time, as she sneaked a glance at Ben. The overhead light threw his cheekbones into sharp relief, making him look mysterious and handsome. Carole shivered slightly, wondering if Stevie was right. Maybe it *was* a bad idea to think there could ever be anything special between her and Ben.

Then again, maybe not. She had seen something in his expression the day before when he'd bent over her to check her eye. She couldn't have imagined that, could she?

Sure I could have, she reminded herself, trying to be realistic. *I thought I saw true love in Cam's eyes, too. And that turned out to be totally bogus.*

Still, she couldn't help thinking that it had been different with Cam. True, she had thought she loved

188

him. But had she ever really felt comfortable with him, the way she felt with Ben right that minute?

Not really, she admitted honestly. *With Cam, I always sort of felt like we were playing roles in some romantic movie. It was exciting, it was different, but it wasn't quite real life. Not like this.*

Remembering what she was supposed to be doing, she grabbed a large cardboard box off the next shelf. It contained a jumble of miscellaneous screws, latches, studs, and other small hardware. Ben glanced at her. "Want me to help you sort that?" he asked.

Carole nodded. "That would be great. Thanks." She set the box on the ground between them and took a seat on another overturned bucket.

Anyway, I have to figure it out, she thought, watching Ben surreptitiously as he stood and grabbed a couple of smaller boxes to put the stuff into. *No matter what Stevie thinks, I have to at least give this a chance.*

She felt a mixture of annoyance and guilt when she thought about Stevie's comments the day before. Carole had managed to avoid her ever since—she wasn't ready to talk to her friends about what seemed to be happening between her and Ben. For one thing, she knew they'd never liked him much. He was way too quiet and private for Stevie, and too aloof and borderline rude for Lisa. Besides, if Carole couldn't understand what was going on with her and Ben herself, how could she possibly explain it to anyone else, even her best friends?

All I know is that I like being with Ben, even if we're never anything more than friends, Carole thought, tossing a horseshoe nail into a box. *It's sort of ridiculous, but I'm happier sitting here with him now, sorting little metal thingies into boxes, than I was on any of my big romantic dates with Cam. Even though I loved Cam—or thought I did, anyway—I never really felt that comfortable with our relationship. I was never quite sure what to do or say to him, and I didn't really know what he saw in me, why he loved me so much. Or claimed he did, anyway.* She grimaced at the memory of how cold and hard his face had looked as he'd walked out on her on New Year's Eve.

Ben looked up just in time to catch her expression. "You okay?" he asked, sounding concerned. "Getting tired?"

"No, I'm fine," Carole replied quickly.

Ben nodded and returned his attention to his task. Carole watched him for a moment out of the corner of her eye. Being Ben's friend had never been especially easy. Despite that, she realized that there had been at least one constant in their relationship: She'd never felt as though she had to pretend to be someone she wasn't with him. Their common unconditional love of the horses they worked with every day had given them an instant bond, even if they'd never really acknowledged it to each other. Whatever good or bad Ben saw in her, he saw it in the *real* her. In fact, Carole suspected that Ben probably knew her better than most people did.

She blinked, realizing it was the first time she'd thought about it like that. She and Ben had worked side by side for a couple of years now, and she'd sort of taken him for granted for most of that time. *But the truth is,* she thought, *I'd really miss him if he weren't here. I'd miss him a lot.*

"You sure you're okay?" Ben was looking at her again.

Carole realized that her forehead was scrunched up in concentration as she contemplated their relationship. "Uh-huh," she said, blinking as she snapped out of her thoughts and grabbed a bucket hook out of the box. She gave Ben a sidelong glance. "Um, actually I'm really good. This is . . . um, nice."

"Oh." Ben looked slightly confused. "Uh, okay."

Carole knew she should let it drop. She'd gotten herself in trouble in the past when she'd tried to express her feelings to Ben. But she couldn't resist trying one more time. "I mean it," she said shyly. "I'm having fun hanging out here like this. With you."

She held her breath, half expecting him to stand up and leave the shed, or at least to scowl and turn away. Instead he cleared his throat and glanced down at his hands. "Yeah," he said, his voice even gruffer and lower than usual. "Me too."

Carole's eyes widened in amazement. Was she imagining things, or had Ben just admitted to having some kind of positive feelings about her? "Really?" she blurted out. "Um, you like hanging out here, too? With me, I mean?"

Ben looked decidedly uncomfortable. "Yeah," he muttered, glancing up at her briefly from beneath his lowered brows. "I do." He cleared his throat again, squaring his shoulders as if he'd just reached a decision. "Er, it's been—that is, I've wanted to say so. For a while now."

Carole gulped and set down the bucket hook she was still holding. What was Ben saying? She didn't want to jump to any wrong conclusions, like she had that day at the horse show. But it really almost sounded like . . . "What—What do you mean?" she stammered uncertainly.

"This is—I'm not very—It's hard for me." Ben coughed and shifted his weight. "I don't really know how to say it right."

He paused, and Carole leaned toward him. He couldn't back away from this conversation now—she couldn't stand it. "Just say it," she urged him. "What is it, Ben?"

"Carole." He lifted his head and looked at her

straight on. "It's just—I—well, I think we've been holding back for too long. That is, I have." He took a deep breath. "I—I like you. Not just as a friend."

Carole gasped. Those were the words she'd never thought she'd hear him say. And, she realized, they were the words she'd been waiting to hear, even before Cam had come along. "Me too!" she choked out. "I like you, too. I can't believe—I mean, I thought you—I didn't think you felt that way."

Ben shrugged awkwardly. "I did," he said. "I have. For a while now."

"But that day at the horse show," Carole began before she could stop herself. She blushed, but she figured there was no point in holding back now. "When you—when we—"

"I know," Ben interrupted with a pained expression. "I—It was an impulse. Something I'd thought about doing for, well, a while."

"But afterward you acted like you wished it never happened," Carole said, confused. "It was like you wanted to totally ignore it."

Ben bit his lip. "Yeah," he said, his voice quiet and raw. "I was stupid. I thought—well, I didn't want to take advantage. Not then, when you had enough to deal with. So I backed off."

"Oh." Carole's eyes widened. Had Ben actually felt *guilty* for kissing her at a vulnerable moment? Was that why he'd acted so weird afterward? Now that she thought about it, that sounded like something Ben would do. If only she'd been able to see that sooner! She felt like the world's biggest fool. Or at least one of the top two.

I can't believe we wasted, like, two months dancing around each other like this, she thought, shaking her head slightly in amazement. *If I'd just had the guts to confront him back then, or if he'd been able to tell me any of what he was feeling, we might have been together all along.*

"What?" Ben was gazing at her anxiously. "Um, what are you thinking about?"

Carole laughed ruefully. "I was just thinking that we're really two of a kind," she said.

"Oh." Ben looked a little confused.

Carole wondered what he was thinking. She thought about asking him. Then she had a better idea.

Okay, Ben was awfully brave to speak up like that when he didn't know how I'd react, she told herself. *Now it's my turn to be bold.*

Scooting her bucket a little closer to Ben's, she leaned over and kissed him. And this time he didn't even try to get away.

Callie pressed her back against the stall wall, feeling a bucket hook digging into her shoulder. She was already wishing she hadn't entered after seeing

George in there. But she hadn't been able to resist checking what he was feeding to her horse. It had turned out to be nothing more than carrot chunks, but somehow, as soon as she'd entered the stall, George had managed to position himself between her and the door.

For the past ten minutes he had been babbling on and on about Scooby, his own schedule, and even the weather while she stood frozen in place, too shaken by his sudden, unexpected appearance to form a coherent sentence. ". . . and so after I realized you weren't home, I figured I'd stop by and see if you were here."

Callie blinked, trying to pull herself together and focus. "You—Wait. You were at my house tonight?" she asked. Scooby blinked and lifted his head slightly at the sound of her voice. The horse had been drowsing in the corner of his stall since finishing off his snack.

George turned to pat Scooby as the horse snuffled at him curiously. "Uh-huh." He shrugged and smiled, as if dropping by to visit Callie at home were the most natural thing in the world. "All the windows were dark, and I thought you might be asleep. But when I climbed up that fence across the street, I could see that there was no one in your bed."

Callie gasped, horrified. "You peeked in my bedroom window?"

"I wouldn't call it peeking." George sounded slightly offended. "I was just checking on you. I was worried, Callie. You know I care about you, and I want to protect you."

Callie's head was spinning. *Oh my god,* she thought. *He's crazy. He's actually truly crazy.*

"Listen, George," she said carefully, her fingers digging into the wooden partition behind her. "We talked about this earlier, remember? How you weren't going to bother me anymore?"

"Oh, it's no bother." George beamed. "I mean, did Superman ever act like it was a bother to keep saving Lois Lane? Nope. Because he loved her. Just like I love you and you love me. You know we're going to be together, Callie. It's meant to be."

"No, it's not!" Callie snapped, feeling panicky. "I don't love you, and I never will. You've got to get that through your head, George."

Instead of looking upset or angry, George smiled. "I love it when you say my name, Callie," he said huskily. He took a step toward her. "You know, it's good that we ended up here together tonight. I was getting tired of playing your game, and now we can just drop it. Right?"

"Wrong." Callie wasn't sure what he was talking about, but she didn't like it. "I'm not playing any games. I meant what I told you earlier."

"Yes, darling." George smiled at her indulgently. "That's what I love most about you. Your spirit."

Callie bit her lip, wondering what to do. She'd never seen George like this before—he was totally over the edge. There was no telling what he'd say or do next, and Callie realized it was pointless to try to reason with him. She just had to figure out a way to get away from him. Obviously her scream hadn't been loud enough to reach Max's house at the top of the hill behind the stable. And there wasn't likely to be anyone else within earshot, not this late at night.

Face it, she told herself grimly. *There's no one close enough to hear me scream again if George—*She paused in mid-thought. What? What was she expecting him to do? He wasn't a monster or an ax murderer. He was just a pathetic, lovesick loser who thought he was Superman.

That thought gave her a dash of courage. "Listen to me, George," she said sternly, gathering her wits and realizing that it was up to her to get herself out of this mess. "I want to get out of here. Step aside and let me pass. Now."

To her surprise, George obeyed immediately, backing off until she could dart past him. She hurried into the aisle and breathed a sigh of relief, feeling much better immediately.

George followed her out, looking slightly sulky.

"I don't know why you're acting like this, Callie," he said in a hurt voice. "I enjoy playing these little cat-and-mouse games as much as you do, but enough is enough."

"Get real!" she snapped, fed up with the whole situation. "There's no game. I really do want to get away from you."

She stepped forward to fasten the latch on Scooby's stall. As soon as she turned her back on George, she heard him step toward her. A split second later, before she could react, his hands were gripping her shoulders tightly.

"What are you doing?" she cried in alarm.

"Hush," George hissed in her ear, his hot breath on her neck. "Don't fight it, Callie. You know this is meant to be."

Callie struggled to get away, but George had her trapped against the stall door. Pressing his body against her, he nuzzled her neck, his wet lips leaving slime trails on her bare skin as he tried to turn her head toward his.

"Stop!" Callie shrieked, twisting her head away. "Get off me!" Managing to get one elbow free, she jabbed him in the ribs as hard as she could.

"Ouch!" George exclaimed, sounding annoyed. "Callie, what are you—"

Taking advantage of the momentary loosening of his grip, Callie stomped on his foot and then elbowed him again, this time in the neck. As he staggered back, crying out in pain, she shoved past him and took off, racing down the aisle as fast as she could. She didn't even realize she was crying until she tasted salt in her mouth.

"Callie!" George called after her. "Wait! Stop!"

But Callie didn't slow down as she took the corner into the entryway. She wasn't going to stop running until she'd left him behind.

"Are you sure you don't want to stop for ice cream?" Scott asked, taking his eyes off the road just long enough to shoot Lisa a smile. "We could go to that place you like. TD's, is it?"

Lisa hesitated. It was still early—barely ten o'clock—and she certainly wasn't in any hurry to get home. She wanted to give her mother's griper friends plenty of time to clear out before she returned. But she wasn't really hungry, and she definitely wasn't in the mood to walk into another public place with Scott. "Maybe we could just hang out at your house for a while instead," she suggested. "You said your parents are out for the evening, right?" Realizing what that might sound like—she definitely didn't want Scott to get the wrong idea—she hastily added, "I haven't seen much of Callie lately, anyway. I wouldn't mind saying hi to her if she's home."

"Knowing Callie, she's probably still at the stable." Scott grinned, then glanced at the dashboard clock and shrugged. "Actually, I'm only half kidding," he added. "Mom and Dad are out tonight, and Callie told them she'd be at the stable all night so they wouldn't drag her along and make her play the politician's daughter. Mind if we stop in and see? It could save her a cold walk home."

"Sure, no problem," Lisa agreed quickly, pleased at the idea. She really doubted that Callie would still be at the stable—by that time of night, the horses almost always had the place to themselves. But it might offer her just the right private setting to talk to Scott about how she was feeling about their relationship. Because the more they went out, the more it felt as though other people were always getting in their way. Barely two minutes had gone by all evening without someone rushing up to them, wanting to say hello to Scott. It was getting downright annoying, but Lisa wasn't sure what to do about it.

Is that just something I'll have to get used to if I want to be with Scott? she wondered again, shooting him a sidelong glance as he drove. *Because I'm not sure I can do it. I'm not sure I'll ever adjust to sharing him with the world every time we go out.*

The stable was only a couple of miles away, and before long Scott was spinning the steering wheel to turn into the long gravel driveway. The nighttime spotlights were on, as usual, but the place looked totally deserted. Lisa glanced at the parking area, which seemed to be empty except for the stable's trailer and truck. Then she blinked in surprise, noticing the corner of a dark red fender peeking out from behind the trailer.

"Hey," she said. "Isn't that Carole's—"

"Callie!" Scott exclaimed.

Lisa followed his gaze. He was staring in the opposite direction, toward the stable. Callie was running toward them, coatless, her long hair flying behind her and her face pale in the spotlight's beam. When she got a little closer, Lisa saw that her expression was wild and frightened.

"What's—" she began, but Scott didn't seem to be listening. Slamming the car into park, he leaped out almost before the motor stopped and ran toward his sister.

Lisa unhooked her seat belt and followed more slowly, confused. What could possibly make Callie look like that? Had she had an accident with her horse?

Callie had her face buried in Scott's shoulder. She was sobbing and babbling. Lisa couldn't understand most of it, but she heard the name George.

Huh? she thought. *It almost sounds like she's saying that George attacked her or something.*

She shook her head, figuring she must have misunderstood. Shifting her weight awkwardly from one foot to the other, she glanced at Scott, wondering what to do.

Scott murmured some soothing words in Callie's ear, stroking her hair as she hugged him tightly. After a moment, he gently loosened her grip and turned her toward Lisa. "Go with Lisa, okay?" he said softly. "She'll take you to the car."

"Is she . . . Is she okay?" Lisa asked hesitantly, stepping forward.

Scott glanced over his shoulder at the stable building. When he turned back to face Lisa, she saw that he had been transformed into a stranger, his jaw set grimly and his blue eyes hard and unfamiliar. "Get her to the car," he said tightly. "Stay there and wait for me." Without waiting for an answer or even giving Lisa a glance to see if she understood, he turned and strode toward the stable, his fists clenched at his sides.

Lisa stared after him for a second. Then, realizing that Callie was shivering in the cold night air, she took her by the arm and steered her toward the car. Opening the passenger door, Lisa stood back to let Callie climb in. Scott had jumped out in such a hurry that he'd left the driver's side door open. Lisa walked around and pushed the seat forward, climbed into the backseat, then shut the door.

Callie had stopped crying. She was huddled in the front, silent except for an occasional sniffle. Lisa twisted her hands in her lap, wishing she knew how to help. How could she, though, when she had no idea what had happened?

After a few more seconds of silence, Lisa cleared her throat. "Um, what's going on?" she asked Callie hesitantly. "What happened? Is George . . . Is George hurt?"

Callie just shook her head. She didn't turn to look at Lisa, and she didn't say a word.

Lisa wait for several long, silent moments. She opened her mouth to ask another question, but then closed it again. Callie's silence was making her feel strangely afraid.

She turned to glance at the darkened stable building. What had happened in there? Before she could begin to figure it out, she saw Scott emerging. He was alone, and as he walked toward the car, Lisa saw that he had a rag wrapped around his right hand. His expression was still grim.

He opened the door and slid in, glancing at Callie with concern. "You okay?" he asked.

Callie sniffled and nodded. "I just want to go home," she whispered.

"We're on our way." Scott started the car.

Lisa sat quietly in the backseat, feeling confused and a little queasy. What had happened between

Callie and George in the deserted stable? What had Scott done just now to injure his hand? She had no idea, and part of her didn't even want to know.

I can't believe this is happening, she thought, turning to stare out the window as Scott's car sped along the darkened country road. *It's like in a movie or something, when everything just suddenly changes. Except I don't even know what actually happened.*

It didn't take long to reach Lisa's street. Scott pulled to the curb in front of her house, then put the car into park without shutting off the engine. He hopped out and pulled the seat forward, reaching for Lisa's hand to help her as she clambered out awkwardly.

"Good night, Lisa," he said distractedly, leaning down and giving her a perfunctory kiss on the cheek. "I'll call you."

"Um, okay. Thanks. And I hope—I hope everything's okay." Lisa wasn't sure if he heard her or not. He was already getting back into the car. A second later he peeled out, leaving her standing alone on the sidewalk.

FIFTEEN

"All right, Ms. Forester," the gentle-voiced female officer said, jotting down a few final notes on her pad. "That should do it. Thank you for answering my questions. I realize it's difficult for you, but we really need to have all the information."

"It's all right," Callie said. "I mean, you're welcome. I understand."

Standing up, she followed the officer into the sparsely furnished room down the hall where her parents and Scott were waiting. Callie had been wavering between embarrassment and relief ever since Scott had bundled her into the house, where they'd found that their parents had just arrived home. Fifteen busy and confusing minutes later, the entire family was on the way to the police station in Willow Creek. At first Callie had been aghast at the whole idea of involving the police—she just wanted to forget the whole thing had happened. But her parents had been firm, and at last she'd given in. It just seemed easier to go along with them, especially since she was suddenly so very, very tired.

She was still embarrassed about what had happened, but surprisingly, telling her story to the officer had actually made her feel a little better. Everyone at the police station was taking her story very seriously, which was kind of a relief after her weeks of solitary worry.

"Is everything okay?" Mrs. Forester jumped to her feet, her face pinched and anxious, as Callie entered and flopped into a chair. Congressman Forester stood as well, putting a comforting arm around his wife's shoulders as he glanced worriedly at Callie.

The female officer stepped forward. "Yes, Mr. and Mrs. Forester," she said calmly. "Your daughter and I had a good talk." She greeted another officer who had just entered. "Let's discuss how to proceed."

Scott scooted over to the seat beside Callie's as the adults huddled near the door, their voices low and serious. "Are you okay?" he whispered.

"Yeah." Callie glanced at him, then poked at his wrapped hand. "Are you?"

Scott shrugged and grinned weakly. "I'll live." He cleared his throat, his smile fading. "But listen. I just want to apologize. You tried to tell me about how George was acting, and I guess I just—"

"It's okay," Callie cut him off. "Don't beat yourself up about it."

"But I should have seen it," Scott insisted. "I mean, you did tell me he was bugging you. I just didn't realize how bad it was getting."

Callie sighed. "To be honest, I didn't quite realize it, either," she said. "I knew it was really getting weird, but I guess I sort of figured it was my fault."

"What?" Scott frowned. "Why would you think that?"

Callie shrugged. "You know. Like, because I wasn't clear enough with George in the beginning. Maybe even led him on." Scott was already shaking his head, but Callie held up her hand to stop him from saying anything. "I know. I know now. He was really out of control tonight, and no way did I do anything to cause that." She shuddered as she remembered how crazy George had acted at the stable. "I didn't believe he had it in him."

"Yeah," Scott said quietly, squeezing her arm comfortingly. "I guess none of us did."

Callie leaned against him for a moment, taking comfort in his solid presence. Then she sighed and glanced at their parents. "So what do you think happens next?"

"I expect they'll take out a restraining order against George," Scott said.

Callie winced. That sounded so serious. What

would people think when they heard about it? What would it do to life at school, at Pine Hollow?

Whatever happens, I'll just have to deal with it, she decided, leaning back in the uncomfortable plastic chair and closing her eyes, soothed by the soft murmur of the adults' voices as they continued their conversation. *Anyway, at least now I know I wasn't going nuts. And maybe now that other people know, now that I have help, I can put this whole crazy nightmare behind me at last.*

Carole was still feeling giddy and breathless as she and Ben made their way up the path to the stable's rear entrance. It was very dark, with only a little bit of light spilling toward them from the nearest outdoor floodlight. Still, Carole was pretty sure that wasn't the only reason Ben had her hand tightly clutched in his own.

I can't believe this is happening, she thought with a shiver. *It's so amazing. Like everything just suddenly changed, and I'm not even sure how or why. But I do know that I like it. I definitely like it.*

She was so wrapped up in her new thoughts and feelings that it took her a moment to notice that Ben was staring at something beyond the stable building. "What?" she asked, following his gaze. She frowned as she saw weird red flashes lighting up the edges of the roof. "What's going on?"

"Let's go see," Ben said grimly.

Carole followed as he hurried around the building. For a moment the only thing she could think about was that he'd dropped her hand. Then she forgot about that as they rounded a corner and saw two police cruisers parked in the stable yard, their blinkers casting an eerie red glow over the familiar scene, making it all look strange and off-kilter.

"What's going on?" Carole asked again, feeling panic rising in her throat. Why were the police there? Had someone broken into the stable while she and Ben were distracted in the shed? Had someone pulled the fire alarm outside the stable office? Had one of the horses gotten hurt somehow? A dozen horrible possibilities flashed across her mind, but she forced herself to stay calm.

Several officers were just climbing out of their cars. When they spotted Carole and Ben, they walked toward them.

Carole swallowed hard, trying not to feel nervous. Despite the fact that she'd never broken a law in her life—she didn't even speed—whenever she encountered a police officer, she started worrying that she'd done something wrong.

"Can—Can we help you?" she asked the officers politely, her throat tight.

One of them, a portly man with a kind face, tipped his hat. "We're looking for a young man name of George Wheeler," he said in a soft drawl. "His folks seemed to think he might be here."

"Oh!" Carole glanced quickly at Ben, then turned back toward the officer. "Um, he was here earlier. But I think he left. I'm not sure."

At that moment she noticed a figure hurrying down the hill. Max.

"Good evening, officers," the stable owner said as he strode over to join the group. He quickly introduced himself. "Is there something I can help you with? Is there some sort of problem here?"

"Not at all, Mr. Regnery," the officer replied. "We just had a tip that someone might be here. Thought we'd stop by and see. Young fellow name of Wheeler."

"I see." Max's face turned grim. He turned to Carole and Ben. "Have you two seen George in the past couple of hours?"

Carole hoped it was dark enough to hide her blush. She and Ben had been out in the shed for a couple of hours. "No, Max," she said as Ben shook his head. She glanced at the officers again. "But what's going on? Why are you looking for George?"

Max shot her an unreadable look. "Go on home, Carole," he said firmly. "I'll sort this out. It's none of your concern."

Carole drew back as if she'd been slapped, even

though Max hadn't sounded angry. She glanced uncertainly at Ben, who was listening quietly.

"Come on," he said, pulling her away by the arm. "Let's get out of their way."

Carole allowed him to lead her toward her car, which was parked beyond the cruisers. "But what's going on? What if George is hurt or something?"

"If he was, they'd know where he is," Ben replied simply.

Realizing that he'd stopped a few yards from her car, Carole hesitated. Ben lived in a poor part of town, and she knew he was a little sensitive about it. "Um, can I give you a ride?" she offered uncertainly.

Ben bit his lip and hesitated. Then he nodded. "Yeah," he said. "Thanks."

Soon they were in the car, heading through the darkened, empty streets toward Ben's house. Carole couldn't seem to stop thinking about the police visit. "Why in the world would the police be looking for George?" she asked. "I mean, he's hardly the ax murderer type."

Ben shrugged. "You never know about people."

Carole was silent, thinking about that. She supposed he was right—and she wasn't just thinking about George anymore. *Who ever would have guessed how this night would turn out?* she thought. *First Ben and I—*She broke off the thought, suddenly feeling shy, almost as if Ben could read her mind. *And then, on top of that, this thing with the police . . . It's been quite a night.*

Before long Carole was pulling to a stop at the curb in front of the small, ramshackle house Ben shared with his grandfather. "Well, here we are," she announced, suddenly feeling awkward. She glanced at Ben, who was unhooking his seat belt. "Um, I'll see you tomorrow," she added shyly, trying not to let it sound too much like a question.

Ben met her gaze. "You can count on it." He leaned over, taking her chin gently in his hand and kissing her softly. Then he turned and let himself out of the car.

Carole watched until he'd walked across the tiny yard and let himself in the house. Then she put the car back in gear. She hated to drive off—to put an end to their wonderful, magical, amazing night.

But she was already looking forward to tomorrow.

Stevie rested her chin on her hands, gazing at the chemistry formula in her textbook. If she stared at it long enough, maybe it would start to make sense. So far, however, that theory didn't seem to be working.

So much for my bright idea to spend a perfectly good Friday night doing homework, she thought, rolling her eyes. She'd hoped to get her school assignments out of the way early that weekend, since she planned to spend all day Saturday and Sunday at the stable. *I should've known better than to go against the laws of the universe like that.*

She was about to get up and see if her brother was home—maybe he had some clue about the homework—when the phone rang. Grateful for the interruption, Stevie hurried to her bedside table to pick it up. "Hello?" she said. "I hope this is the chemistry fairy, 'cause I could really use some help."

"Stevie?" Lisa's voice sounded tight and disturbed.

"Lisa? What's wrong?" Stevie asked, instantly concerned. "You sound weird."

"That's because something weird just happened," Lisa said.

Stevie perched on the edge of her bed. "Tell me," she demanded.

"It's Callie," Lisa said. "Scott and I stopped at Pine Hollow to see if she was there. We were just in time to see her run out, looking all freaked out and scared."

Stevie gasped. "Why? What happened?"

"That's the thing. I don't know." Lisa sighed noisily into the phone, sounding worried and frustrated. "Callie wasn't exactly in a chatty mood."

"But what happened?" Stevie clutched the phone

tightly, not wanting to miss a single word. "I mean, what did you guys do?"

"Scott went marching in there, all furious and everything, and came out like five minutes later with his hand bandaged," Lisa said grimly.

Stevie wrinkled her nose. She was having a little trouble following the conversation. "What, you mean like a Band-Aid?"

"No." Lisa's voice was somber. "It was more like a polo wrap or something. It was all wrapped around his hand—you know, like his *fist* was sore."

"Oh!" Stevie let out a low whistle, finally understanding what Lisa was telling her. At least some of it. Just then the doorbell rang. "Oops. Can you hold on? Someone's at the door." She glanced at her watch as the bell rang again, surprised. It was after ten, and she wasn't expecting any company.

"Hi," Carole said breathlessly when Stevie swung open the door. "Sorry it's so late."

"Hey, that's not your fault," Stevie joked, though her heart wasn't in it. "Come on in. I have Lisa on the phone—sounds like something weird went down at Pine Hollow tonight."

"Tell me about it," Carole said as she stepped inside and unzipped her jacket. "I just came from there."

"Really?" Stevie glanced at her watch again in surprise. It was pretty late to be just leaving the stable, even for Carole. But she didn't worry about that for

214

long. She was more interested in whatever had happened. "So spill it. What's the deal? Lisa said Callie was all freaked out, and then Scott—"

"Huh?" Carole looked confused. "No, I was talking about the thing with the police."

Stevie was already leading the way back upstairs, not wanting to leave Lisa hanging. "What?" she asked. "The police were at Pine Hollow?"

"Uh-huh. And they were looking for George Wheeler."

Stevie blinked. None of this was making sense. "Pick up the extension there," she told Carole, pointing to the phone in the hallway. "I'll get it in my room."

Soon all three of them were on the phone. Lisa filled Carole in on what she'd just told Stevie, and then Carole explained what she'd just witnessed. When they were finished, Stevie was more perplexed than ever. "It sort of sounds like it all must be related somehow," she said slowly. "Like maybe George was bothering Callie again, so Scott beat him up—Wait," she interrupted herself. "Then the police might be looking for Scott, not George."

"They were definitely looking for George," Carole put in. "Maybe they want to see if he wants to press charges against Scott. If it really did happen like Stevie just said, I mean."

"I guess," Lisa said dubiously. "I don't know,

though. Callie really looked upset. Like, more than just bothered, you know?"

Stevie sighed. "Well, I guess that's the main thing we need to know," she said. "Callie's our friend, and whatever the heck happened over there tonight, it sounds like she might need our friendship right about now."

"Right," Lisa agreed.

"Definitely." Carole sighed. "I just can't imagine. . . . Well, I guess we'll just have to wait and find out what happened."

There didn't seem to be much more to say, so they hung up. Stevie walked Carole to the door and said good-bye, then headed back upstairs. Flopping onto her bed, she stared at the ceiling and mulled over what Lisa and Carole had told her. It seemed impossible that George—the shy, gentle, friendly guy who wanted to help her improve her riding, the person she was just getting to know better—would do anything that might get him in trouble with the police. Then she thought about Callie, and remembered the pale, frightened look she'd had when George had tried to join them in the restaurant, the reluctance she'd shown when George wanted to come along on the trail ride, his constant presence at Pine Hollow whenever Callie was expected, his disappearance when Callie left. None of it had seemed like much to

Stevie, but it might have been a lot to Callie. An awful lot.

"Oh, no," Stevie said out loud. "What did I miss? What did we all miss? Just when Callie needed us the most . . ."

She wondered if she should just call Callie—see if she was all right, find out the truth about George. But glancing at the clock on her bedside table, she saw that it was pretty late.

I'll wait until tomorrow, Stevie thought reluctantly. *And I'll be there for her. We all will.*

ABOUT THE AUTHOR

BONNIE BRYANT is the author of more than a hundred books about horses, including the Pine Hollow series, The Saddle Club series, The Saddle Club Super Editions, and the Pony Tails series. She has also written novels and movie novelizations under her married name, B. B. Hiller.

Ms. Bryant began writing The Saddle Club in 1986. Although she had done some riding before that, she intensified her studies then and found herself learning right along with her characters Stevie, Carole, and Lisa. She claims that they are all much better riders than she is.

Ms. Bryant was born and raised in New York City. She still lives there, in Greenwich Village, with her two sons.